UNDER YOUR BED
13 TALES OF TERROR

CHILLING TALES FOR THE CAMPFIRE
BOOK TWO

BLAIR DANIELS

CONTENTS

The Painting My Husband Keeps	1
Hide And Seek	13
There's Something Wrong With My Childhood Photos	18
The Virtual Interview	33
My Girlfriend's Texts Don't Sound Like Her	38
Thou Shall Not Steal	52
Hotel California	64
Someone Is Living In My Fairy Garden	78
I Was Invited To A Swinger's Party	90
My Neighbor's Backyard	102
Why We'll Never Go To Mars	115
My Husband Dies Every Night At 7:48Pm	128
A True Crime Podcast... About Myself	135

THE PAINTING MY HUSBAND KEEPS

When my husband and I first got married and moved in together, we had a few fights. On personal space, on chores... and on décor.

Namely, my husband insisted on keeping this weird painting of a woman.

"Who is she?" I'd asked when I first saw it, leaned against a mountain of moving boxes.

"Dunno. Got it at a rummage sale."

It was an original painting. Oil, I think, judging by the way the light reflected off the brushstrokes. It depicted a young woman standing in a dark room, looking over her shoulder at the viewer. She was actually rather beautiful. Blonde hair falling over her shoulders like a waterfall. A white cotton dress. A dainty, heart-shaped face that was somehow haunting rather than cute.

She was illuminated brightly, but the room behind her was dark. The contrast and her pose reminded me a little bit of *Girl With A Pearl Earring*. But it didn't feel classy, or pensive, or beautiful. Instead it felt... creepy. Especially because my husband insisted on hanging it above our bed.

"I mean, it's a beautiful painting," I said. "But it just doesn't fit with the modern décor."

"Neither do your Funko Pops."

"Okay, but they're small. This painting is *enormous*. For Pete's sake, the woman is nearly life-sized!"

"I want to keep her where she is."

It seemed like a big deal to him, so I dropped it. But it wasn't easy. Sometimes I woke up in the middle of the night with the horrible feeling that I was being watched. Then I'd look up and see her haunting gray eyes staring down at me.

I didn't get much sleep after that.

And there was the one time I swear she moved. "Was her hand always like that?" I asked Eric, after getting into bed one night.

"Hmm?"

"Her left hand. The fingers are kind of open, reaching out behind her. Like she's waiting for someone to grab her hand."

"Yeah, she was always like that."

I could've sworn she *wasn't* always like that. Then again, I generally avoided looking at the painting. It was so uncomfortably realistic. When I stared into those gray eyes, I almost felt like I was making eye contact with a person.

I lasted two weeks. Then I begged Eric to move it.

"Can we *please* move the painting somewhere else? I really hate looking at it when I'm going to sleep."

"It's the nicest piece of art we have. It belongs above the bed."

"What about the sunflower one?"

"That's just a print," he complained. "And it's so basic."

"Come on. I'll move my Funko Pops out if you move the painting out."

He heaved a long sigh. "Fine. I'll move her."

That was another thing. He often referred to the painting as "her." It was weird.

So he moved it to the stairs. But honestly, that was worse. Every time I went downstairs, there she was. Staring at me from above the landing with those piercing gray eyes. At least when the painting was in the bedroom, I was usually asleep or facing the opposite direction.

I hit my breaking point a few days after that.

For some reason I couldn't sleep. After tossing and turning for an hour, I decided to grab a snack downstairs. I got to the top of the stairs... and there she was.

I hadn't turned on the main lights—only the nightlight in the hall bathroom was on. With everything so dark, the background of the painting melted into the shadows. But the woman still stood out, with her pale face and white dress.

And my stupid, sleepy brain interpreted it as an actual person standing there.

I jumped about a foot in the air. And I would've

fallen all the way down the stairs, had I not caught the banister at the last second.

"Can we pleeeease get rid of that painting?" I asked the next morning.

Eric turned away from the stove, set the spatula down. "Why?"

"Last night, it scared the frick out of me. I nearly fell down the stairs."

He stared at me, as if unable to understand. "She... scared you?" he asked slowly.

"Well, more like startled me. I thought it was actually a person standing there."

He looked at me.

Then he broke into laughter. And, after a few seconds, I started laughing too. It *was* pretty stupid, now that I thought about it. I know I was sleepy, but still—I thought the painting was a *person?!* What, did I think we were being burglarized by a young, beautiful, blonde woman in a nightdress?

"For now, I'll move her into my office. Then you don't have to look at her at all."

"That sounds good."

And for a while after that, things were okay. I sort of noticed Eric spending more time in his office than usual, but he also had a big deadline for a brief coming up. And what, how would that be related to the painting, anyway? It's not like he was staring at her for hours on end.

Except that's exactly what I caught him doing.

One night he didn't come downstairs to eat dinner with me. I called up to him a few times. No reply. So I went upstairs and walked into his office—to find him staring at her.

He was just sitting there. With his computer closed. No papers on the desk. Swivel chair turned towards the woman in the painting.

"Oh," he said suddenly, when I walked in. Then he quickly stood up. "I was just about to come down. Just sent in the brief a few minutes ago. They're really happy with it."

He smiled broadly at me, as if nothing were wrong, and then slipped past me. I listened to his footsteps thump down the stairs.

Had he actually just finished working?

Or was he just sitting in here... staring at her?

I ultimately decided not to bring it up. The painting was out of my sight and that was great. Besides, I had bigger fish to fry, like my own deadline coming up for an article I hadn't even started.

But then, on Friday afternoon, I accidentally overheard him on the phone. His voice was muffled through the thick wooden door, but it wasn't hard to hear him. He was shouting, almost.

"I'll have it in by tonight—"

"No, I knew it was due on Wednesday—"

"Well, my wife fell down the stairs. I had to take her to the hospital."

Those words sent a chill through me. I barged in.

"Why are you lying about me falling down the stairs?"

His face paled. He ended the call and turned towards me. "I'm so sorry, Tara. But I needed an excuse.

I missed the deadline on that brief, and it's my job on the line—"

"The brief you told me you finished two days ago?"

He nodded, silently.

I crossed my arms. "Look, Eric, your work is your business. But we've spent, like, all of one hour together all week. Because you've been locked in here all day, every day. I mean, are you even working? Or are you just sitting in here, staring at *her?*"

His dark eyes locked on mine. And then his voice grew soft.

"You're jealous of her."

"... *What?!*"

"You shouldn't be, Tara," he said, stepping towards me. "The painting makes her prettier than she was."

I froze. Stared at him.

Then I finally found the words. "Are you saying... this is a painting of someone you know?"

"No," he said slowly. "Sorry, I misspoke. I meant, whoever this is a portrait of, I'm sure it's a flattering likeness. All portraits are flattering like that."

I stared at him, my heart pounding in my chest. "Who is this a painting of, Eric?"

"I told you, it's not—"

"Eric." I stepped towards him. My legs felt weak, wobbling underneath me. "*Who is this a painting of?!*"

He only shook his head.

I couldn't sleep that night.

I know, it sounds silly, being so worked up over a painting. But you have to admit it was weird. He was obsessed with this thing, for whatever reason. *Why didn't I see the painting when we were dating? Did he hide it away in the basement?* That was the one place I'd never been. Had he built a little shrine down there, painting, candles, the whole nine yards?

The thought of it made me sick.

Is it an ex-girlfriend? An ex-wife, even, that he never told me about? Getting a painting commissioned must have cost a fortune. Especially a huge, detailed one like this. I mean, as much as I hated that thing, it was clearly done by someone incredibly gifted. The glint in those piercing gray eyes, the small dimple on her right cheek...

But clearly he wasn't keeping it to appreciate the artistry.

He knew her.

And whoever she is, he's obsessed with her.

And then I got the craziest idea.

I sat up in bed. Slowly, quietly. Turned to Eric. He was fast asleep. Then I slipped out from underneath the covers, grabbed my phone from the nightstand—and tiptoed out of the room.

My bare feet padded softly across the hallway as I made my way towards his office. Then I pushed the heavy wooden door open and stepped inside.

The office was cold—much colder than our bedroom. Goosebumps pricked up my bare arms. But I didn't waste any time. I reached over, fumbling across the wall, and hit the switch.

The light flicked on.

The blonde woman stared down at me from the wall. Her eyes seemed to follow me as I took Eric's leather chair and dragged it across the hardwood. Once against the wall, I stepped up onto it.

We were staring at each other, face to face.

I'd never been this close to the painting before. My face inches from hers. This close, I could truly appreciate the detail. Each individual eyelash painstakingly drawn, curving up from its follicle. Threadlike striations of light and dark gray filling her irises. Her skin, so pale and creamy, dotted with the tiniest of pores.

But I wasn't here to appreciate the artwork.

I lifted my phone—and took a photo.

Then I brought up a reverse image search.

It took a few minutes for me to find the right website and upload the photo. But when the results loaded... I gasped.

I expected maybe one result, if I were lucky. Some sort of facial recognition that would match the painted face to a photo. Or, maybe the artist's website would come up, and mention who the subject was. But instead —*dozens* of thumbnails filled the page. Of the exact same painting I'd been staring at for weeks.

Fingers trembling, I clicked on the first one. It led to a news article.

Search Continues for Missing Franklin Art Student

My heart dropped. Little black dots danced in my vision. I collapsed into the chair behind me, trembling, and began to read.

Anya Kelsing, 23, went missing after a hike with her boyfriend...

The two became separated when they came upon a bear...

Her backpack was found roughly a mile from where the sighting occurred, but no trace of Anya was found...

And the caption under the painting.

Kelsing is a third-year student at Franklin College, majoring in Fine Arts. She recently completed a self-portrait that was exhibited at Le Coeur (above)

I clicked on the next article, and the next—but they all said the same thing. Hike, bear, disappearance. All of them showed a photo along with her self-portrait; she looked strikingly identical to her painted likeness. None of them mentioned the boyfriend's name, but it had to be Eric. The most recent article, from five years ago, was a video clip of her parents begging for her search to continue. Sadly, judging by the news articles, it never did.

I don't know how long I sat there. All I know is that I was suddenly jolted from my thoughts by a loud *thump* in the hallway.

Footsteps. Coming towards the office.

I shot up. *He can't find me here.* I glanced around the room, looking for someplace—any place—that I could hide. But it was probably too late. Surely he'd seen the light on, from under the door...

I ducked under the desk just as he stepped into the room.

"Tara?"

I clapped my hand over my mouth, trying to silence

my ragged breathing. *He's going to see the chair out of place. He knows I'm here. He knows...*

"Tara, you in here?"

Why did I hide? I could've just said I came in here because I heard a noise. Needed a pen. Couldn't sleep. Why the fuck did I hide? Now he's going to know that I know...

"Tara?"

But maybe it's fine. Maybe the bear got Anya, maybe Eric had nothing to do with it. Isn't that more likely than Eric being a murderer?

"There you are."

I looked up—and screamed.

Eric was crouched there, in front of the desk, staring at me.

"I—I was looking for a pen," I stuttered, lamely. "I wanted to write down—I remembered I have to pick up groceries tomorrow and I needed to add something..."

He tilted his head, a small smile on his lips. "I don't think that's the truth, Tara."

Make a break for it.

I started to lunge out from under the desk. His hand quickly shot out and grabbed my wrist. *Hard.* "You figured out who she is, didn't you? That's the only reason you'd be hiding from me."

I trembled in his grasp. "What did you do to her?" I whispered.

He let out a dry laugh. "So you think I'm a murderer. How nice, that's the first conclusion you jump to."

"No—no, I don't think you're a murderer." I swallowed. *Stupid, stupid, stupid. If he killed her, and he knows you know... then you're dead too.* "I'm sorry. I didn't mean that. Just... what happened? They didn't find a body. Did the bear get her?"

He didn't reply. Just stared at me, silently, with those cold dark eyes.

"I was jealous," I continued, desperately, "but now I understand. I wish you'd just told me. To lose someone like that... of course you'd want to keep the painting. It's all you have left of her."

"You should have just left it alone," he said, his tone oddly emotionless. "I'm sorry you had to find out this way."

I screamed as he lunged for me.

It's over. His hands were clenched tight on my wrists as he dragged me out from under the desk. I pulled back, trying to wrench myself free, but it was no use—

Thump!

A loud crash sounded behind us. Eric whipped around, and for a split second—his grip released.

I acted instantly. Pulled free from him and ran, pivoting around the desk and racing towards the door. As I glanced back, I saw Eric, starting after me.

But I also saw what had made the noise.

The painting of Anya had fallen from the wall. It lay askew on the floor, her gray eyes staring emptily upwards.

I was always a fast runner.

Eric was only halfway down the stairs by the time I was at the bottom. Bursting out into the cold air, I began to scream. He grabbed me from behind and tried to pull me back inside, but it was too late. Lights were flicking on. Our neighbor rushed out of his house, dialing 911.

It was over.

The police arrested Eric for assault. And once I told them my story, of his obsession with Anya's painting, they were able to search our house. And hidden in his office drawer, in a small box, was a pair of gold earrings.

The same earrings Anya wore on the hike that day.

The case is slowly mounting against him. I'm hoping, praying Anya gets justice and that a jury convicts him of her horrible murder.

And would he have done the same to me, if I hadn't escaped? If Anya's painting hadn't fallen off the wall?

There was an explanation, of course. When Eric had moved the painting to his office, he'd mistakenly installed one of the hangers into pure drywall. The weight of the painting had caused it to rip out, and the painting fell.

But sometimes, I think Anya was watching over me. That her self-portrait carried a piece of her. And that night, she'd protected me from falling victim to the monster who ended her life.

The painting now hangs up in my foyer. Every day I walk by it, and new details pop out at me: the deep, shadowy green of the room behind her. A perfectly-painted strand of blonde hair. The glint in her piercing gray eyes.

And sometimes, I think she's smiling back at me.

HIDE AND SEEK

During quarantine, my four-year-old and I played a lot of hide and seek. Well, hide and seek with a few extra rules: (1) I'm the only one that hides (he doesn't want to), (2) I have to call out "Yoo-hoo!" every few minutes (otherwise he'd never find me), and (3) when he gets close, I pop a hand or foot out of my hiding spot. And he shrieks "I SEE YOUR FEET AHAHAHAHA!"

Four-year-olds are really stupid, okay?

And I didn't exactly have the money to buy him a ton of toys. We'd just moved into this house a few weeks ago. The rent took up nearly my entire paycheck. I got all the furniture from Freecycle, we ate beans and rice often, and I was still driving around a twenty-year-old car.

"Hide again," Benjamin said, tugging my hand. "Hide again!"

"But it's almost bedtime."

"Pleeeeease?"

"Okay. But only one game, okay? Go count in the kitchen."

He ran around the corner as fast as he could. "1... 2..." I ran through the living room, and then I saw it: the hall closet. Perfect. I opened the door and ducked inside. It was a tight fit—all those scratchy, furry old coats pressing against me—but it was worth it.

Because the better the hiding spot, the more time I got to myself.

I pulled out my phone and started browsing Reddit. Soon his muffled footsteps sounded, around the dining room. I waited a minute; when he didn't seem to be coming my way, I cracked the door.

"Yoo-hoo!" I called out.

Footsteps grew louder. I heard his muffled giggles as he walked towards me—and then he started going up the stairs.

What an idiot. I cracked the door open a little further, just in time to see his little feet disappear from the landing. Then I shrugged. *More time for me.* I sat back down in the closet and pulled out the phone.

"Mommy," I heard him giggle from upstairs. "Mommy, where are you?"

I smiled. *I wonder if a mom invented hide and seek. It's quite brilliant. You get a few precious minutes away from your child, and they're not even supposed to make much noise. But you're entertaining them at the same time! Absolutely br—*

"Yoo-hoo!"

I stopped.

Every muscle in my body froze. But I heard it, clear

as day. A soft, clear voice calling from upstairs. But Benjamin and I were home alone.

Oh God someone's in the house and Benjamin—

I burst out of the closet. "Benjamin? *Where are you?!*"

I heard Benjamin's footsteps running above me. His giggles, trailing down to me. I couldn't move. Couldn't breathe. "Benjamin!" I finally screamed.

More giggles. And then Benjamin's voice:

"I SEE YOUR FEET!"

No. I catapulted up the steps, screaming for him. I burst into his bedroom—but he wasn't there. Just his empty rocket bed, comforter rumpled, embroidered stars staring back at me. I ran back into the hallway, spinning around.

"*Benjamin?!*"

But I didn't hear any footsteps. Any giggling. The house was dead silent now, and I could hear a pin drop. I ran into the guest bedroom. It was empty. I ran over to the closet. Threw it open, looked up and down.

Nothing.

Stumbling back out in the hallway, I crossed back towards my bedroom. The only bedroom left. I ran inside and flicked on the light.

Empty.

The pile of dirty laundry on the chair—untouched. The wardrobe—hanging open, my clothes inside. The pillows piled up on each other in a heap. Heart dropping, I ran around the other side of the bed. Also empty. I crouched to look under the bed. Empty.

"Mommy? Mommy?"

Relief flooded me as I heard that voice. The door to

the bathroom opened a crack, and one blue eye peered out at me, wide with fear.

I ran over and grabbed him. Hugged him. And then I hoisted him up and started out of the bathroom.

His eyes were still wide with fear. And they weren't focused on my face, but the spot just over my shoulder.

I whipped around. It took me a moment to see it... but then I did. I stared at the wardrobe, frozen, my heart pounding in my ears.

In the shadows, poking out from underneath the hems of my dresses and coats, were two feet.

In moments like this, the brain doesn't really think. It's too slow. Instinct reigns. The smartest thing would have been to lock ourselves in the bathroom and climb out the window. But instead—I just ran for the hallway. As fast as I could.

As I ran down the stairs, I heard the weighted footsteps, slow and methodical, resonating through the house. I could still hear them pounding into my brain as I ran to the neighbor and screamed for help.

The police came. They searched the house. They didn't find anything—no signs of forced entry, either. So they promised me they'd patrol my street for the next few days, but that was really all they could do. I decided to stay at a friend's house for a few weeks, until I felt safe again.

But every time I closed my eyes, I could see them. Those two feet, that looked so *off,* somehow. Swollen, as if waterlogged. A bit too grayish in tone to belong to any normal person. Toenails blackened and split.

And I think back to that wardrobe. How I'd gotten it

for free. How the owner told me his mother had just died, and he was just trying to get rid of all her stuff as quickly as possible.

And I wondered.

How, exactly, *did* she die?

THERE'S SOMETHING WRONG WITH MY CHILDHOOD PHOTOS

I found it while cleaning out the closet.

An old photo, creased at the corners. It depicted a little boy sitting on a chair in the middle of a wallpapered kitchen. Blue eyes, blond hair. I flipped it over and checked the date on the back. November 14, 1996. So me, when I was four.

Except...

The kid didn't look quite like me.

The photo was grainy, so it was hard to tell for sure. But the eyes were a little too wide set. The smile was too toothy.

So, a friend? But it was definitely my mom's kitchen. Floral wallpaper with pink rosettes, the old oak table. And the kid so closely resembled me... wouldn't I remember having a friend that looked like he could be my twin brother?

And why isn't it with the other family photos?

I'd found it in Mom's closet. She had several photo

books, all populated with childhood photos. Documenting the most insignificant events, from baking cookies to baseball games.

So why wasn't this photo with the rest?

Why was it hiding on the top shelf of my mom's closet, tucked under a hatbox?

I walked out into the family room, grabbed the photo album labeled *1995-1998*. Paged through it until I got to a good, clear photo of myself at four.

Then I pulled the photo from my pocket and compared the two.

It wasn't a great comparison. My head was tilted to the side, and his was straight; I was wearing a hat, he wasn't. Still—the difference was unmistakable. His grin was wider, toothier. His skin was paler. His eyes were wider set.

Yet, the differences were subtle. To anyone but me, they'd probably look like the same person.

"What are you doing?"

I turned to see my mom, standing in the doorway, carrying a large box.

I hesitated, wondering if I should bring it up to her. She had enough on her mind, with my stepdad passing away and the big move. "I found this photo. Who is that?"

She set the box down and walked over. "That's you! When you were four or five." She smiled. "Aww, how sweet. Look at you."

"But it doesn't..." I hesitated again, knowing I would sound crazy. "It doesn't, um, look exactly like me, does it?"

"Yeah, you were a goofy-looking kid." She laughed. "You got a lot better-looking as you aged."

"No, I mean, that photo doesn't look like I did when I was a kid. Look, see." I held up the photo of me in the Red Sox cap side-by-side with the photo of the boy in the kitchen.

"I think they look identical," she said.

"No, they don't."

"Maybe it's the hat. Hey, can you help me in the attic? There's a lot of stuff up there."

"Sure. I'll be there in a second."

She smiled at me and turned away. I listened to her bare footsteps recede on the carpet. Then I snapped the photo album shut and put it back.

I tucked the photo in my pocket.

Then I walked back into my mom's room and opened the closet.

There were more. When I took down the hatbox to search under it, the top came off—revealing an entire trove of photographs. I picked up a few of them—and my heart dropped.

A kid hunched over a birthday cake with four candles, smiling. Me. Except... *not* me. The same toothy grin, the same wide set blue eyes.

A kid standing in the front yard, pointing to a frog. My front yard. Again, not me.

And then there was a photo that made my heart stop.

A photo of my bed. I still remembered those covers, with the sports cars on them. The pillow with the wheel on it. The car lamp. But there, sitting on the bed—

Not one little boy.

Two.

"Adam?" my mom's voice came from above.

I stared at the photo, frozen. Me... sitting next to a little boy that looked almost exactly like me. A twin? A brother? I had no memory of this kid. All my life, I'd believed I was an only child.

"Adam!"

The stack of photos was a few inches thick. There was no way I could go through them all. I slipped several in my pocket, replaced the hatbox, and then headed down the hall.

"Coming, Mom!"

I started up the ladder—

And my phone began to ring.

The theme to *Legend of Zelda* played its tune. I stopped two stairs up and slipped the phone out of my pocket.

Caller ID: Ali. My wife.

"Yeah?"

"Can you get me a drink, too?"

"Uh, sure," I said. "What do you want me to pick up on the way back? The usual whiskey?"

"On the way back?"

"Yeah. On the way back from my mom's. I'll be here another hour or two, but—"

"You're at your mom's?" she asked. Her voice suddenly soft, confused.

"Yeah, why?"

"I don't understand. I just let you inside the house,"

she said. "You're down in the kitchen. Making us drinks. ...Aren't you?"

The phone slipped from my hands.

I stumbled down, snatched it up. My heart pounded in my ears. "Ali—that's not me. I think I have a twin. You need to lock the doors—"

"A twin? Adam, that's—"

"Ali?"

His voice.

It sounded just like mine. Yet, there was something *off* about it; something I couldn't quite place. Like listening to a slightly out-of-tune piano.

"*Lock the door!*" I shouted into the phone.

A heartbeat of silence. Then hurried footfalls as she ran over to the door. *Click.*

"You locked it?" I asked, weakly.

"I did." Her voice was trembling.

I crumpled against the wall, relief flooding me. "I'm going to call the police, okay? But if you can get out the window—or something—"

"Adam!" my mom shouted down from the attic. "Are you coming up, anytime this year?!"

"Just a second!" I shouted back.

"Ooookay," she said, skeptically.

I pressed myself into the closet. Must filled my nose as I pulled the doors shut in front of me, pressing me in. "Ali? Are you still there? Are you okay?" I whispered.

"I'm trying to get out the window," she whispered back. "It's a long drop, but—"

Muffled knocking sounds, through the speakers.

"Ali?" I heard him call. I shuddered. Hearing him say my wife's name made my skin crawl.

"I'm calling the police. Do anything you can to stay away from him."

I disconnected the call and dialed the police. When I was assured they'd send someone over, I took a deep breath and opened the closet door.

And froze.

Mom was standing right outside.

"Who were you talking to?" she demanded.

I stepped back, rustling against a row of sweaters. Fear swept through me, but then curiosity—anger—took over.

"I have a twin brother."

Her eyes widened. Then her face crumpled, and she closed her eyes. "I never... never... how did you—"

"He's at my house. Right now." I pushed past her.

"He's with Ali?" She clapped a hand over her mouth.

That told me all I needed to know.

"You need to call the police," she called after me. "I did," I shouted back, as I ran down the stairs. I pulled the phone out of my pocket and dialed Ali's number again. Five rings, then went right to voicemail.

I ran into the driveway. Yanked open the front door, dove inside. Mom got in the passenger seat.

"Mom—"

"I know him better than anyone," she said, not looking at me.

The engine rumbled to life underneath us. I screeched out onto the road. A few minutes of silence passed between us. Then she spoke.

"I did it for your safety."

I scoffed. "For my safety. Yeah, right. And now my wife is at the hands of... what? An evil twin? A psychopath?" I swung onto the highway, pushing my foot on the accelerator. "Why did you *really* tell me all my life that I was an only child?"

"Because you are."

"Mom—"

"I only gave birth to one little boy." She took in a shuddering breath, then let it out. "*He* showed up on our doorstep one day, when you were about four. Nowhere to go. Your father—being religious and all—wanted to take him in. He said the poor little boy got lost in the woods, and it was our duty to care for him until his family was found. So we adopted him."

"That doesn't even make se—"

"Let me finish," she snapped, with sudden anger. "We contacted the police, everyone, trying to locate his family. All our searches turned up empty. It was like he'd just—just popped out of thin air." In my peripheral vision, I could see her turn to me, her expression grim. "And that day, we took him in... I swear he didn't look a thing like you."

"I don't understand."

"The change was so gradual, it was hard to notice. In the span of year, his hair went from brown to blond. His face went from gaunt and pointed to round and full. And whenever I brought it up with your dad, he was always so defensive about it. *He's been playing in the sun a lot. He was so skinny when he got here; he's gained weight, of course that's going to make his face look different.*"

A drizzle started, flecking the windshield with bits of rain. I turned on the wipers. They squeaked against the glass.

"Then your dad started saying things that didn't make any sense. Like, one time I ordered a big lunch at Arby's. He laughed and said, *are you eating for three again?* And he'd say here and there, *when you were pregnant with the twins...* it was like he truly believed Alaric was our genetic son."

With a shaking hand, I clicked on my turn signal and veered towards the exit. "Why don't I remember him? Was there some sort of traumatic event, or—"

"You still don't remember the day your father died, do you?"

"No. He... he fell down the stairs, didn't he?"

"I'd left you and Alaric with him while I went to the grocery store. When I came back ..." Her voice cracked with emotion. "You were crying. You didn't remember anything. Alaric, on the other hand... well, he was acting like an angel, like he always did. But he had this *smile* on his face." She let out a breath. "I knew he had something to do with it. Even though he was just a child... I can't explain it. I just *knew*. So I put him up for adoption and tried my best to erase him from our lives."

Her words hung heavy in the silence.

"So... I don't remember him because of Dad?" I finally asked.

"I don't know." She let out another shaking breath. "I was so worried, how I was going to explain it all to you. You'd just lost your father, and now you were losing your brother. But it was the strangest thing. The day he left our home... you forgot he ever existed."

"Wow." I stared at the rain pelting down, running across the windshield, then swiped away by the wipers. My hands felt tingly and numb on the wheel. Nothing made sense.

"Ali's still not picking up," Mom said, tapping at her phone.

"Doesn't matter. We'll be there in a minute."

I swung onto our street. As the houses flashed by, my heart pounded faster. *Ali... please be okay...* The little blue colonial came into view, with the hydrangeas and two garden gnomes. I pulled into the driveway, halted to a stop. Pushed open the door and ran inside.

"Ali?" I yelled.

The house was quiet. *Too* quiet.

"Ali!" I screamed.

I raced up the stairs, Mom running behind me. Turned the corner.

The door to our bedroom was wide open.

"No, no, no."

Shards of glass littered the floor. A puddle of whiskey stained the carpet. The window was open, curtains fluttering in the breeze.

But the room was empty.

"He's got her. Oh, God, he's got her."

I sunk to my knees. The world reeled around me. *If he killed my dad...* I couldn't bear to think of the horrible things he would do to my Ali. Tears stung my eyes. *I have no idea where they went. No way to find out. No way—*

The *Legend of Zelda* tune filled the room.

Slowly, with shaking hands, I picked up the phone.

"Ali! Where are—"

"He wants you to come here."

She was sobbing. Distant *thumps* sounded over her tears—footsteps, pacing around her. My heart plummeted.

"Where are you?"

"If you come here, he's going to kill you," she whispered. "I don't—I don't know if you sh—"

"*Where are you?!*"

"At—at the old arcade," she whispered. *Click*—the line went dead. I pocketed the phone and looked up at Mom, frozen by the window.

"He wants me to meet him."

Her eyes widened. "No! No, you can't!" She grabbed my arm and clung to me, pulling me back as I tried to step out of the room. "He'll kill you. And he'll somehow get away with it. And—"

"He's got Ali, Mom. I don't have a choice."

I ran down the stairs, then ducked into the basement. I opened our small gun safe and pulled out a revolver.

Then I said goodbye to my mother.

We hugged in silence on the driveway, to afraid to actually speak the words. Then, with one last wave, I peeled out of the neighborhood.

The arcade had been abandoned for at least a decade. Weeds popped up in the cracks of the parking lot, slowly crawling towards the building. Chunks of brick crumbled off the exterior and the windows were broken, shards of glass rising up like pointed teeth. A tilted, stained sign still read *Neon Arcade*.

Chain-link fencing surrounded the condemned building—but the gate hung open.

I pocketed the revolver. Then I walked towards the building, slipping through the gate. A raven *cawed* and took flight.

I entered the building.

The inside was dark. The only light came from a large hole in the the ceiling over an old Pacman machine. I slipped my hand in my pocket, fingers wrapping around the gun. "I'm here," I called out, my voice echoing in the dust. "Now give me Ali."

A strangled whimper from somewhere behind me.

I whipped out the gun and reeled around—but there was only darkness. Only rows of dusty old video games that would never see another player. Only a claw machine filled with moth-eaten animals, faded beyond recognition.

"Alaric!" I shouted.

A rustle.

And then Ali burst out in front of me. She stumbled into the aisle, her hands tied behind her back, a gag over her mouth.

I ran to her, untying her wrists as she cried behind the gag. As soon as they were free, I pressed my keys in her hands. "Run. Take my car. Get as far away as you can. And—"

She ripped the gag off.

"*He's behind you, Adam!*"

I wheeled around.

I was looking at... me. Yet it wasn't me. The man standing in the darkness of the arcade was the same height as me, with the same skinny build. But the way he stood so still, staring at me with gleaming eyes... that wasn't me.

I'm not sure it was even human.

"Go," I whispered to Ali.

"I can't—"

"*Go!*"

She gave me one last, pleading look before running out of the arcade. I turned around to face Alaric—

The aisle was empty.

I reached into my pocket and pulled out the revolver. I held it in front of me, aiming, my hands shaking.

"Looking for me, Adam?"

He was standing *right behind me.*

I was staring into my own blue eyes. Although, this close—with his face inches from mine—I could see slight differences. Just like in the photographs. His eyes were a hair too far apart. His cheeks were slightly thinner. He was missing the scar on my chin, that I'd gotten falling off a bike in fifth grade.

And then he grabbed me.

Pain shot through my body as he shoved me to the ground. The gun slipped out of my hands, skittered across the floor. His lips—*my* lips—twisted into a horrible smile. Before I could move, he was crouching down to the stained carpet, reaching for the gun—

"No!"

Ali's voice.

No, no, Ali—

I lunged forward and grabbed the gun. "Ali, *get out of here!*" I screamed as I stumbled up. I whirled around, but I couldn't see either of them. Rapid footsteps sounded in the next aisle—but I had no idea who they belonged to.

And then—silence.

"Ali?" I whispered, my voice shaking.

Silence.

"Alaric?"

Thump.

Motion caught my eye.

But what I saw in my peripheral vision was not Ali—or Alaric.

It was tall. Incredibly tall. Its fur, or skin, was pitch black—the color of the sky on a moonless night. Its arms hung at its sides, so long they nearly dragged on the floor. And its face... its face was a scrambled mess of human features. Several eyes, all different colors, blinking rapidly. Two mouths, oriented vertically. Opening like gills on the side of its face.

Then my eyes focused on it—and the creature instantly condensed into my own form.

I took a deep breath. Aimed.

And pulled the trigger.

Snap.

Alaric stumbled.

And then he collapsed. I ran over to him, panting, the revolver shaking in my hands. A stain grew on his chest—but it was a deep, colorless black. Not red. He looked up at me, with *my* blue eyes, and his mouth twisted into a smile.

Then he fell still.

It's been almost six years since that day at the arcade.

Ali was waiting for me outside, unharmed. Despite the loud gunshot, the police never showed up at my door. But I did see a little article a few weeks later, tucked away on a local news website. Some urban explorers broke into the arcade and found tufts of fur and bones that weren't easily recognizable. Being reasonable people, they'd turned the stuff over to the local cryptid society instead of, you know, a lab or something.

Now there's a resurgence of bigfoot sightings in our town.

But life for us has been pretty amazing. Ali and I sold our house and moved a few towns over, to a rural little cottage nestled in the woods. And then we found out we were pregnant. Now we have an incredible four-year-old named Ava and two tabby cats, Anna and Elsa.

You can guess who named the cats.

Sometimes I think back to that day. What would have happened if Alaric killed me. Our wonderful little Ava never would have been born. Ali would've been a widow. Or—even worse—maybe Ali *wouldn't* have been. Maybe Alaric, or whatever that thing was, would've come back home and pretended to be me.

Just the thought sends shivers up my spine.

"I'm going to bed," Ali says, leaning over to kiss me. "Are you sure you can't come up?"

"Nah, I have to finish this. It's due on Monday and you know I'm not going to get any work done tomorrow, with my mom visiting and all."

She grins at me. "Your mom is such a good grandma."

"Ha. She spoils Ava a little, if you ask me."

Ali laughs and heads up the stairs. I listen to her footsteps fade, then transform into the sound of creaking boards above me. I sigh and turn back to my computer.

It's near midnight when I hear it.

Thunk, thunk, thunk.

Three knocks at the front door. Soft and polite. I frown, slowly getting up from my chair. *Did Mom decide to come tonight, instead of tomorrow morning?* She'd surprised us a few times like that before. But never so late at night...

I walk over to the door and peer through the peephole.

My blood runs cold.

It's a little girl, standing on our porch. Hands tucked into her pockets, humming to herself. Smiling as she stares at the door. Dark hair, pale skin.

And about four years old—just like Ava.

THE VIRTUAL INTERVIEW

I'm an alumni interviewer for my alma mater. This year, we've been conducting most of our interviews online. It's been a lot of fun.

Until I got Casey.

On paper, Casey looked like a great fit for our college. Great ACT scores, lots of extracurriculars, and some prestigious art awards.

But as soon as she joined the video call, I knew it wasn't going to go well. She was using one of those awful beauty filters. *During an interview!* And not a basic one with lipstick and eyeshadow—one of those creepy subtle ones, that makes your eyes slightly bigger and your skin unnaturally smooth.

I tried to ignore it. Tried to pretend like she didn't look like some mannequin-woman come to life. "So, Casey, why do you think you would be a good fit for C___ University?" I asked, forcing a smile.

"I love the art program," she said. As she spoke, the

filter seemed to glitch—her mouth moved strangely as she formed the words. *Must be that teeth-whitening filter.* Her teeth were WHITE. Like glowing. Like Ross-from-that-one-episode-of-Friends white.

"Okay. You love the art program... what about it do you like?"

"I love the program's focus on real-life models."

Okay. At least she was prepared—researching our specific program meant she was pretty interested. I jotted down a note: *Seems interested.* "What type of art do you specialize in?"

"I like to paint."

"You like to paint... what, specifically? Portraits, or landscapes..."

"Faces."

"Oh, so, portraits."

"No. I like to paint faces."

She said it in this aggressive tone. Like she was correcting me, and annoyed that I'd made such an egregious error. I almost asked, *what's the difference?*, but then decided it might make me look stupid. "Okay, um, that's really neat." I jotted down—*Likes to paint FACES. Not portraits, FACES.* "Why do you like to paint por—I mean, faces?"

"I think they're fascinating," she replied, her too-large eyes boring into mine.

"Okay. That's good." *Kind of a strange personality,* I added to my notes. "Tell me, Casey—what do you like to do in your spare time?"

For me, this was the perfect barometer of a candidate. Lots of smartass kids would try to outsmart me on this one, and say things like "learn" or "read books" or "try to cure cancer." Others were totally oblivious and answered things like "partying with friends" or "instagram." The really good ones were in the middle; the ones that said things like "hiking" or "playing piano" or "visiting Grandma."

She stared at me for a moment, the light in her eyes strangely elliptical from the filter stretching them out. Then her mouth opened, lips moving strangely over her too-white teeth.

"I like to paint faces."

"But what *else* do you like to do in your free time?"

She paused, her face blank. Almost like she was confused by the question.

"Do you maybe like to hike, or hang out with friends, or—"

"Faces are just so fascinating to me," she interrupted, her tone soft. "The way the nose protrudes from the cheeks. The way the eyes glisten in the light."

"Uh—"

"The way the mouth stretches and curves, showing so many different expressions," she continued, her tone growing faster. Frenzied, almost. "The emptiness of the forehead. The intensity of the eyelashes. The curve of the chin, the—"

I held up a hand. "Yes, uh, I understand. You like to paint faces. But can you, uh…" I trailed off. This girl was really weird. Half of me just wanted to click the "end call" button right now, with no explanation. But I had a duty, right? A duty to fairly interview this girl and write up a letter about her to the admissions committee.

"Here. How about this. If you had the next twenty-four hours off and unlimited money, what would you do?"

She smiled. Lips stretching to show off those bright-white teeth. "I'd paint a face," she said, smiling wider by the second. "*Yours.*"

Chills crept down my body. "... What?"

"I'd paint *your* face," she continued. "I've been looking for a new one. And yes... the brightness of your blue eyes, the curl in your hair, the soft lines around your eyes that show wisdom... it's perfect. Perfect, perfect, per—"

I clicked end call.

And then I sat there, half-terrified and half-perplexed, staring at my desktop. My fingers still on the touchpad, ice cold.

I filed a police report and did everything in my power to find "Casey." But I got no answers. It was like she didn't even exist outside her college application and our little interview. Even the main admissions office couldn't track her down. They told me all her application materials had been anonymously filed, the metadata on her documents completely wiped.

I slowly convinced myself the whole thing was a dumb prank. She probably put the whole interview on TikTok or something. Kids these days.

It was three weeks after our interview that I found it.

While on a video call with a friend, I noticed a filter

I'd never seen before. With a name that was a string of random characters, a thumbnail that was a blank screen. And I can't help but wonder... if it's watching me, studying me.

    Learning to paint my face.

MY GIRLFRIEND'S TEXTS DON'T SOUND LIKE HER

My girlfriend went hiking. Her texts don't sound like her and I think something is terribly wrong
Posted to Reddit on Saturday, September 4th, 6:17 PM by R_____

Reddit, you have to help me. Please. I don't know what to do.

Today, my girlfriend Thea decided to go hiking. I know--I should've gone with her. But she always does her hikes alone because I slow her down. Usually she's only gone two hours or so.

Now, she's been gone for nearly four.

I'm considering calling the police. She should've been home by now. I've tried calling her, repeatedly--but she doesn't pick up.

All I have is our text conversation from the day, and as I read it over and over I feel like something is terribly off.

2:33 PM
Me: Seen anything cool yet?
Thea: Nope. I'll send you pics when I get to the waterfall tho!!
2:57 PM
Thea: You're cooking dinner tonight right?
Me: Yep! Chicken pot pie
Thea: Yum!! So excited!!

After that interchange, we didn't exchange any texts for about an hour. I wiled away the time constructing pylons in *StarCraft*.

Then, around 4, she sent me a text.

4:06 PM
Thea: I found the waterfall!!

Below this text was a selfie.

Thea, standing in front of a small waterfall, smiling at the camera. Arms crossed, cap covering her wild hair. Earrings--the turquoise ones I'd given her on our first anniversary--glinting in the light.

I sent a text back.

Me: You're cute ;)

Then I stopped.

Something about the photo... bothered me. I stared at her smiling face, blue eyes shaded by her cap. Her thick curls of black hair, brushing her shoulders.

Wait.

Her arms were clearly crossed. She wasn't holding the phone--there was no way she could be.

Someone else had taken the photo.

Or maybe she'd propped it up on a rock or in a tree.

But she couldn't have taken the photo herself. I quickly shot off another text:

Me: Who took that photo?

She didn't reply to that, right away. So I'd left the phone on the desk and went downstairs to start prepping dinner. I pushed the creeping anxiety to the back of my mind and focused on the food, putting more effort than usual into cutting the onions.

Call me paranoid, but my last girlfriend cheated on me and left my heart broken. Knowing someone else took that photo--and the fact that she hadn't responded to that text, when she'd responded to the others promptly--made me feel awful.

Come on. She probably just asked some passerby to take her photo.

*Clunk--*my knife sliced through the onion, hitting the cutting board with a full thump.

But what if...?

When I got back upstairs forty-five minutes later, I was relieved to see there was a new text.

4:53 PM

Thea: thinking of you ;)

I frowned. First, she didn't answer my question. Second, Thea doesn't usually send emotes or smileys. Gifs, sure, but not this.

It was weird.

Me: Thinking of you, too. Did you get my last text?

Thea: i'll be back by dinner time <3

Thea usually didn't send less-than-threes to me

either. That was more me. In any case, I decided to let it go.

Me: Ok. I love you. <3

I unpaused *StarCraft* and played for a while. I was only interrupted by my phone pinging. I picked it up.

A text.

5:37 PM
Thea: i'm on my way back
Thea: *[image loading]*

The image popped up.

It was another selfie. This time, she was holding the phone--I could see her outstretched *arm* in the lower part of the frame. And she was standing in a much clearer part of the forest--she must've been near the trailhead.

I breathed a sigh of relief and began to type.

Me: Awesome! Pot pie is already in--

My fingers froze.

In the photo--just at the edge of the screen--there was something in the fallen leaves.

A shadow.

A shadow, just a few feet from her own, cast by someone off screen.

It's after six now. Dinner is cold. I've been sitting here, my heart pounding, calling Thea repeatedly.

Nothing.

Except for one text that came in, as I was typing this up.

Thea: i'm going to be home late. sorry. i love you <3

Somehow... I'm sure she wasn't the one who sent that text.

Posted Monday, September 6th, 11:53 PM by R_____

Sorry I didn't post last night. So much has happened, and I'm still trying to process everything. I guess I'll start at the beginning.

Thea never returned home on Saturday night.

A lot of you told me to go look for her myself. So that's what I did—after I called the police, I headed over to the trail alone. (Well, not entirely alone; I brought our little dog, Gisele, thinking she might be able to pick up a scent or something.)

But as soon as I pulled into the parking lot, my heart dropped. There was her car—her beat-up Honda civic—parked crookedly under a streetlamp.

Thea's still here.

But she wouldn't do that. Not voluntarily. It was already pretty dark out, and we have a lot of coyotes in the area. She wouldn't be stupid enough to keep hiking past dark.

Would she?

I tried the door to her car—locked. Shined my phone's flashlight in the windows. She wasn't in there. Nothing looked out of place, though it was hard to tell with how messy Thea's car always is.

The dread in the pit of my stomach grew. I grabbed Gisele and headed towards the trail.

As soon as we stepped into the woods, it was even

darker. What little light was left in the sky was choked out by the thick foliage. I took a second to glance at the sign, to figure out which way the waterfall was.

Then I continued into the forest.

"Thea?" I called. "Thea!"

No response.

I looked at Gisele. She didn't seem to be picking up anything. I tried to call Thea again. She didn't answer. All I had was that last text, staring me in the face:

Thea: i'm going to be home late. sorry. i love you <3

As a last-ditch attempt, I sent a text back.

8:23 PM

Me: How late? Where are you? I've been calling you.

I watched as the indicator went from *Sent* to *Delivered*.

And then to *Read*.

My blood ran cold.

My fingers flew over the keys, starting to type. *Where are you? Please call me...* But then I stopped. If it really wasn't Thea writing those texts—if it was someone who *had* her—maybe that wasn't the smartest thing. I stood there in the middle of the woods, my heart pounding, as Gisele whimpered at my feet.

And then I typed.

Me: That's fine if you want to stay out late, but I'm going to bed. I love you. Goodnight.

Three little dots appeared in response.

And then it popped up.

Thea: no you're not

I stared at those three words, my head swimming. *Huh? What does that mean?* Gisele pawed the ground a few feet away.

And then another text came in.

Thea: you're out here looking for me
i hear you calling my name
why don't you come a little closer ;)

I grabbed Gisele, and broke into a run. Over the thick roots and large stones. The terrain sloped up, then down. Out of breath, I stopped, shining the flashlight in a circle around myself. "Thea!" I screamed, straining my ears for something—anything—that might sound like her. A rustle, a footstep, a sound. *Anything.*

But there was nothing.

I pulled out my phone and sent another text.

Me: WHERE IS THEA?

And then, finally—I did hear a sound.

Pa-pa-ping!

That strange little tone. The one I'd heard all over the house for the past two years. Whenever Thea got a text or an email.

It was Thea's phone.

Right out there, somewhere, in the darkness.

I blindly ran towards the sound. But as soon as I stepped off the trail, the terrain changed. A deep slope, a carpet of dry leaves. I hadn't gone ten steps when I stepped on the uneven surface of a jagged rock. My ankle buckled—I lost my balance—I careened into the darkness.

Thud.

Then a rustling sound off to my left.

The snap of a branch.

I pulled myself up as fast as I possibly could. Pain shot up my ankle, but I continued blindly forward, waving my phone every which-way. White light flashed across gnarled trunks, yellowed leaves. Gisele barked at me from the trail.

But I didn't see anything.

I sent Thea another text.

Me: TELL ME

And then I listened.

But there was no *pa-pa-ping!* No footsteps, no rustling. Nothing. Just silence, punctuated by Gisele's barks.

The police arrived soon after that. I told them everything. I showed them the texts, showed them where I'd heard Thea's cell phone. They didn't find her—but they did find something in the parking lot that I'd missed.

A turquoise earring.

I didn't sleep on Saturday night. I drove around town for hours, looking for anything suspicious, asking late-night partygoers if they'd seen anything. I called the police repeatedly, checking in on their search.

Nothing.

And then, when the sun broke over the treetops, my phone pinged. To my surprise, it was Thea.

6:42 AM

Thea: i'll see you soon :)

Thea: [image loading]

A selfie popped up.

But this one wasn't like the others. The photo was dark and grainy. The forest was all grays and shadows, maybe taken just after sunset or just before dawn. And there, leaning against a tree... was Thea. Arms hanging at her sides. Hair wild. Her cap pulled so far down, her eyes were completely hidden in shadow.

Just looking at it made me feel like throwing up.

I sent the photo to the police immediately, but they haven't been able to do anything with it yet. I thought they had some technology where they can pinpoint the location of a cell phone... but either they haven't been able to do it, or they don't want to tell me yet what they've found.

But there's one thing I *haven't* told the police.

Tonight, I got one final text from her. After nearly 48 hours without Thea, after my fruitless search in the forest, after everything the police have done. This is all I have. One final text.

11:46 AM
Thea: are you going to come find me? ;)

I think maybe it's time to return to the woods.

Posted Friday, September 10, 6:27 PM by R_____

You guys pointed out that going into the woods was a bad idea. You're absolutely right. When I wrote that, I'd had maybe 2 hours of sleep and about 5 cups of coffee. I wasn't thinking clearly.

That text was a trap, set by whoever took Thea.

I handed everything over to the police. Even the final text. They were able to find out what cell tower Thea's phone was pinging off of—but, unfortunately, the area encompassed most of the park. I organized a small search party to go around town and search. We also posted all over social media.

Everything came up empty.

Wednesday rolled around with no texts, no leads, no word from the police. And then Thursday. Each hour that went by without hearing anything, I got a little less hopeful. Several times I forced myself to look at those three photos she sent me, to look for clues. But they only made me feel sick.

And then Friday happened.

I'd started the day as usual. Checked in on the social media groups, looking to see if anyone found anything out. I made some coffee and was about to call the police to see if there were any updates—

And then my phone rang.

When I saw the caller ID, I couldn't believe it.

Thea

I snatched the phone and immediately picked up. "Thea?" I asked, my heart pounding in my chest.

Silence on the other line.

"Thea, tell—tell me where you are. Please."

Silence.

"If this is who took Thea... please. I'll do anything. Don't hurt her. I'll pay ransom, I'll do whatever you want. Just—please, please don't hurt her."

No one spoke—but I did hear something, now. A faint crackling sound. *Static? The wind blowing through the speakers?*

"Please, say something!"

My heart pounded. My legs shook. I glanced around

the kitchen, my mind racing. *Can't the police trace the call? Do they need to be on the line? Do I need to keep the call on for 60 seconds?*

I had no idea.

"Do you want money?" I asked, my voice trembling as I opened my laptop. "We don't have much but I'll wire it all to you. Right now. Please, just give Thea back to me." I began placing a wireless call to 911.

The crackling sound intensified.

"Please—"

The call dropped.

I immediately told the police. Begged them to trace it, to do something. But they just gave me the same canned responses they had for the past several days.

So I got in my car and drove.

I didn't even know where I was going. But then I found myself pulling into the parking lot, staring at those same dark trees and winding trail.

I was debating whether I should actually go in when I saw it.

A plume of dark smoke, rising above the treetops.

I jumped out of the car and ran into the forest--all while that horrible crackling sound played in my head. *Thea, no, no...* I climbed over rocks and sticks, following the acrid smell of smoke. *Please, don't let it be—*

The fire stood in a small clearing—orange flames licking the air, black smoke billowing up to the sky.

Posted Friday, September 10, 10:54 PM by R_____

Thea's remains were found in the fire.

God. Saying that... *her remains*... how can you say that about someone you love so much? Such a crude, horrible thing to say. Thea... my wonderful Thea... is gone.

Since I got the news I've been sitting in the kitchen, downing whiskey as I flip through photos of us in our final days. A photo of us on the boardwalk, her grinning and holding a stuffed teddy bear, me standing stiffly beside her. I remember that trip—how annoyed I was that she wanted to play every game in 90-degree weather.

What an idiot I'd been. Every minute with Thea was a gift.

I flipped to another photo. A selfie of us on the couch. Her grinning as she held up the bowl of pasta we'd made from scratch. My thumb hit the screen as I started to flip to another photo—

I stopped.

Is that...?

In the photo, I could see our front windows behind the couch. I could see the neighbor's lights across the street, see a car rolling by on the road. And... I could see something else.

An irregular shadow.

I zoomed in. The photo quality wasn't great—grainy swaths of blue and gray—but even so, I could see what it was.

A figure.

Crouched between our two bushes. Looking inside.

I stared at the blurry shape, frozen. Then I flipped to

the next photo. Thea and I sitting on the floor a week prior, playing with Gisele. And, zooming in to the window... I saw that same awful shape. Crouched just outside the halo of our back porch light. The next one. The unknown assailant peeking in through an uncovered corner of our bedroom window.

No.

I flipped to the next photo—oh God, no, no. Thea standing in the laundry room, balancing a basket on her head and sticking her tongue out at me. But behind her —*inside the house*—a sliver of darkness poking out from around the corner. Not a shadow, but some*one* standing there—

Yip!

I jumped a foot as Gisele let out a shrill yelp from the family room. I scrambled over to find her sitting in front of the window. Staring into the darkness outside.

Yip!

Shaking madly, I stumbled over to the front door. Clicked the deadbolt into place. Then I cupped my hands over the window and peered out.

Nothing.

I ran through the house, making sure every window, every door was locked. I closed the curtains, even slid the lock across the basement door. Then, knowing I was safe, I collapsed into the couch and began dialing the police.

In a few minutes, they'll be here, and they'll know everything. They'll find the bastard that killed Thea, who has apparently been stalking us for months, and we'll make sure he gets the worst sentence he possibly can. Thea will get justice.

It's finally over.

or has it just begun?

:)

THOU SHALL NOT STEAL

I didn't mean to steal it.

I'd taken my son to the playground, like I always do on Saturday afternoons. He was happily playing in the sandbox when this blond boy came over.

I internally rolled my eyes. It was obvious from the moment I saw him—he was one of the rich, spoiled kids from the prep school down the street. He was holding a beautiful little train engine. One of the Thomas tank engines, I think, with a face on the front. All shiny and new.

He stood right there, in front of my son. Who was playing with a dingy, old dump truck.

"Hi," he said, with a mischievous grin. "Do you want to see my train?"

"Yeah!"

He held it out to Aidan. My son reached for the train. The boy jerked back. "Don't touch it! It's *mine!*"

Aidan's face fell. I looked up at the mom, waiting for

her to cut in. To tell her son to share. Instead, she shrugged. "Sorry. He's very attached to his train."

I stared at her in shock. She looked back at her phone, seeming not to care.

I stood up and grabbed Aidan by the arm. "Come on. Let's play somewhere else." I shot the mom a death glare and pulled him over to the climbing wall.

And that little brat followed us.

A minute later he was standing there, next to Aidan. Waving that stupid train in his face. I glanced over at the mother—engaged in her phone. Not even looking.

"Do you want to see my train?" he asked, again.

"No. No, we don't." And before I could say more, I grabbed Aidan's hand and forced us to walk away.

The kid finally forgot about us after that, and Aidan and I ended up having a decent time. An hour later, it was time to leave. As we walked through the playground, we passed the sandbox.

The train was there, forgotten in the sand.

I turned around. The boy and his mom were at the other side of the park, using the monkey bars.

No. I shouldn't.

But then I looked down at Aidan. My poor boy. He didn't ever get shiny new trains like that. That kid probably lived in a mansion, with a family that looked like they walked off a Lands' End catalog. We lived in a tiny house built in the 1950s. And his father was halfway across the country, doing who knows what (and who knows *who*.)

I knew it was wrong. But I bent down, picked up the train, and slipped it into my pocket.

The good thing about four-year-olds is, even though they ask questions, they're also really stupid.

"Is this the train from the boy at the park?"

"His mommy told me we could have it."

And that was that. Aidan didn't point out the fact that we'd been together the entire time, and there was no way I could've talked to the woman without him noticing.

"Cool!"

Seeing him play with that train made me so happy. He played with it for hours, rolling it along the coffee table, pushing it on the waffle-block train tracks. Then it was bedtime—and only then did he agree to part with the train.

"Did you have fun today?" I asked, as I finished reading him a bedtime story.

"Yes."

"Good. I had fun today, too."

After Aidan fell asleep, I went into the kitchen and poured myself a shot of whiskey. It had been a while since I'd had a drink, but today I needed it. I kicked back in the living room, turning on some *I Love Lucy* reruns on my computer.

Did I do the wrong thing?

The last thing I'd stolen was a pack of gum. In the seventh grade. Stealing as an adult—even if it was from a bratty kid who deserved it—definitely felt *wrong*.

But when I thought of the smile on Aidan's face, the guilt faded away.

You're doing what's best for your son.
I reached over and took another swig of whiskey.
You did the right—
Woo-ooo!

The clear sound of a train whistle cut through the house. I whipped around—and found the tank engine sitting on the coffee table, glinting in the dim light.

Dammit. I didn't know it made noise. Geez, I wouldn't have stolen it if I knew. Aidan was the kind of kid that would press the buttons on his toys over and over until I was ready to stab my ears out. I absolutely hated toys that made noise.

Woo-ooo! the sound came again. Louder than I would expect such a small toy to make. I heaved myself up from the sofa and snatched it up. "Okay, okay… where's the off button?" I muttered to myself, turning it over in my hands.

The face stared up at me, with its pupiless eyes and wide smile.

Up close, it didn't *quite* look like Thomas the tank engine, like I'd thought at the playground. The face was more realistic—the color was halfway between peach and gray, sort of a sickly flesh tone. The nose protruded more, and the eyes were smaller and slightly almond-shaped.

What, didn't that kid have enough money to buy a Thomas branded tank engine? I thought it was only poor moms like me who bought the rip-off toys.

Well, whatever.

I turned it over, then glided my fingers along the plastic. I easily found the small, plastic switch underneath the train. I flicked it off and tossed it into the toy bin.

Then I went to bed.

Woo-ooo!

The next day, I endured hell. That damn train kept going off every five minutes. *Woo-ooo! Woo-ooo! Woo-ooo!* But I'm a good mom. I let him play with it for four hours straight. That's 48 train whistles, by the way. If I were counting. Which I wasn't.

Finally, I managed to distract Aidan with TV. As he sat on the carpet to watch *Cars* for the hundredth time, I snuck away with the train.

I ducked into the kitchen, set it on the table. Then I grabbed a screwdriver and sat down.

Oh yes. I was going to operate on that poor little tank engine—and take his batteries right out.

There was about a fifty-percent chance it would throw Aidan into a tantrum tomorrow. But there was also a chance he wouldn't even notice. After all, he'd played with the train a whole day before even realizing it made noise.

I found the battery panel easily—right underneath the power button. I stuck the end of the screwdriver in. Twisted. The plastic popped out.

I lifted the case.

What?

There were no batteries inside.

Only two cylindrical cavities, where two AAA

batteries should go. Empty springs glistening in the light. *That's weird.* But maybe it could be charged up, too, or had an internal battery for demo modes and stuff like that. Toys kept getting more and more complicated.

I sighed and replaced the battery panel, the screw. Defeated, I handed the train back to Aidan.

Woo-ooo!

It was going to be a long day.

"Aidan, it's bedtime."

He ignored me, pushing the train along the track.

"Aidan, come on."

Nothing.

"Okay, I'm going to go upstairs and read The Little Blue Car without you!"

Woo-ooo!

I charged up the stairs, making my steps as exaggerated as possible. Then I settled into his bed and picked up the book. "Once upon a time!" I read, at the top of my lungs. "There was a little blue car! And he was the smallest car in the whole—"

Thump, thump, thump.

Ah. It worked.

Aidan ran into the room, snuggling down next to me. Without the train, thankfully. I wrapped an arm around him and finished the story, enjoying time actually *together,* instead of just watching him play with that train.

"I want water," he said, when we'd finished.

"Okay! I'll go get you some."

I walked out of the room, down our short little hall, and started for the stairs. I took a step down—

My knees buckled.

Something shot out from underneath my foot. I lost my balance, teetered on the edge for a second, and then began to fall. My arms flailed wildly as the stairs zoomed towards me.

And then my hand caught.

I grabbed the banister. My entire body jerked to a halt. Heart pounding, I looked below. Fourteen stairs. Down, down, down into the darkness below.

And, laying two stairs below me, was that damned train.

The terror I felt quickly turned into anger. I charged back into the bedroom. "You can't leave the train on the top of the stairs like that! I just tripped—I could have—" I stopped myself. "Really hurt myself!"

Aidan stared at the book.

"Aidan? Do you hear me?"

"The little blue car," he said softly, turning a page.

"Aidan! Look at me!" I leapt onto the bed and grabbed his face, making him make eye contact with me. "Don't. Leave. Toys. By. The. Stairs. I almost hurt myself, really badly."

He stared at me.

And then he started crying. A high-pitched wail that echoed through the entire house. I tried to explain, so he'd understand. I hugged him. I told him it was okay, he just needed to be careful.

But all he did was cry.

I couldn't sleep.

Around 2 AM, I finally decided to call it quits and go downstairs for a drink. I walked into the hallway, quietly. Grayish-blue shadows fell across the carpet, extending from the window at the end.

I hesitated, at the top of the stairs. *I could've died.* My gaze fell. The train engine was still there, perched on a stair. The face pointed up at me, still grinning.

I carefully made my way down—then bent over to pick up the train. I continued down the stairs, into the kitchen, and stood in front of the garbage bin.

I don't care how much he cries. I don't care. I'm going to throw it out.

My foot drifted to the lever. I pushed down; the lid popped open. I extended my hand over the trash, holding the train.

And stopped.

What?

In the kitchen light, I could see it clearly. The face was no longer a grayish-pink—it was bright peach. Nearly identical to my own. The eyes were gray, with black pupils. The cheeks had a faint, pink stain on them, and the chin jutted out from the round engine.

My hand trembled.

I released it.

It fell to the bottom of the garbage with a solid *plunk.* Quickly, I pulled the garbage bag out—even though it was only half full—and tied it up. I dragged it into the garage, pushed it into the garbage can, and snapped the lid shut.

I stood there, in the middle of the garage, panting. My heart racing. The cold seeping into the soles of my feet.

And then I heard it.

Woo-ooo!

Muffled, from the depths of the garbage can.

I raced back into the house. Shut the door. Locked it. *Woo-ooo!* The whistle met my ears, faint through the door.

I ran back upstairs. Then I grabbed the old sleeping bag from our closet, walked into Aidan's room, and rolled it out across the floor. I stared up at the ceiling, at his glow-in-the-dark star decals, until I finally fell asleep.

How Aidan cried for that stupid train.

It was tantrum after tantrum. He'd forget about it for maybe an hour, getting engrossed in a toy or a movie. Then, suddenly, he'd stand up and wail: "Where's the traaaaaiiiin?" And crumble into a fit of sobs.

But I didn't waver.

Its horrible little face was still imprinted in my mind. I saw it every time I closed my eyes. Fleshy skin. Rounded nose. Realistic eyes. A never-ending grin.

It had to be my imagination, how it seemed to change. How it looked like any old Thomas the tank engine toy at the playground, but now, resembled a near-perfect human face sliced off and stuck on the front of a train. I must've not taken a close look at it. I never did, with Aidan's toys.

That's what I told myself. And when I heard the telltale *woo-ooo!* coming from the garage—when my heart plummeted—I quickly ushered Aidan away. Of course he screamed. Threw a fit. But it's what I had to do.

Thank God it's garbage day tomorrow.

I was so sick of hearing him cry that I put the garbage out early. Right after dinner, I rolled that trashcan out to the curb. Aidan seemed to get a little better after that. He couldn't hear it, he couldn't see it, and thus it was easier to forget about.

By bedtime, he seemed to have mostly forgotten about it.

"I love you, Aidan," I said, wrapping my arms around him. "You know that, right?"

He nodded. "I love you, too, Mommy."

"Awww. My sweet boy." I squeezed him tight. "Hey. Tomorrow, let's do something real fun, okay? Maybe we'll go to the museum."

"The museum?" He grinned. "Cool!"

"Yeah. Now, go to sleep, sweet boy." I got up from the bed and clicked the door shut. Then I sunk down, under my covers, feeling like an enormous weight had been lifted off my shoulders.

I woke up late the next morning.

The lost sleep from that stupid train finally caught up with me, I thought, as I stretched and yawned. I could tell by the way the light filtered through the curtains that it was at least seven, maybe later. I yawned again and walked out into the hallway.

Aidan's door was open. The bed was empty.

Huh. Usually he ran into my room as soon as he woke up—but sometimes, he'd go downstairs to play with his toys. "Aidan?" I called.

No answer.

I walked down the stairs—and my heart leapt into my throat.

The front door was hanging open.

"Aidan?" I yelled, my voice growing more panicked. "Aidan?" I ran out onto the front steps, despite still being in my pajamas. "Aidan! Where are you?"

And then I saw him.

Stepping into the street.

Towards something small and shiny in the middle.

And then I heard it. A rumble of wheels, a gust of air, a flash of silver metal. A car was coming—barreling down the road. Too fast.

"Aidan! No!" I screamed.

I was running. Flying. But it was too late. He was in the middle of the street, crouched down, picking up the toy.

Screech.

The car braked.

I watched as it came to a screeching halt. Less than three feet from my son.

"Oh my God, I'm so sorry," the woman said, leaping

out of the car. But I didn't listen. I rushed past her and grabbed Aidan. And I collapsed in the street, holding him tight. Sobbing madly.

He wouldn't even look at me.

He was staring at the train in his hands. *Woo-ooo!* the whistle went. A few pieces of wayward trash littered the road and the lawn—had one of the bags burst open? And the train fell out? My head swirled with a thousand explanations.

"I love you so much," I sobbed, gripping him tight.

And then, before the woman could walk over, I grabbed the toy from him. I hoisted him on my chest and carried him back up the driveway, as he started wailing and screaming. The driver kept apologizing, but I waved her on. "It's okay. Please, don't worry about it."

I waved her on, a small smile on my lips as she started the car.

And then it rolled forward. *Crunch*—a horrible sound as the front tire crushed the toy against the asphalt. I saw her frown, and glance around in confusion. I gave her a thumbs up.

Then she was gone. I stood there, admiring the twisted remains of the train. Cracked wheels, crushed engine, and a face split in two. And something oddly dark spilling out from it, shining like oil in the summer sun.

Woo-ooo, came the distorted audio.

Aidan's screams reached a fever pitch.

I smiled.

HOTEL CALIFORNIA

It happened during our spring break trip, our senior year at UCLA.

What I wouldn't do to go back in time and stop that trip. I've replayed it in my head a hundred times. If only Sara hadn't broken up with me. If only my parents hadn't let me use their car. If only I hadn't insisted on driving all night...

Did fate want us there? With all the things that lined up just right, sometimes I think so. If anything went differently—if a fucking butterfly flapped its wings in Antigua—I don't think we would've been here, at 2:45 AM, coasting down a dark desert highway.

Dev reached over and turned up the radio. "Seasons don't fear the reaper," he sang horribly off-key, "nor do the wind, the sun or the rain—"

"Will you *please* be quiet?!"

I glanced in the rearview mirror. Emmett. He was glaring at us from the backseat, his smooth babyface in a deep scowl. A travel pillow hung from his neck, a blanket wrapped around his feet.

"Sorry, did we wake you up?" I asked, with a fake pout.

"Yes."

"Oooh, poor little Emmett is cranky because he missed his eight o'clock bedtime," Dev said, turning around with a devilish smile on his face. "Better get his pacifier and blankie!"

"Fuck you."

Did you know it's scientifically proven that planning a vacation is much more fun than taking one? Now, I know why. Turns out, taking a 500-mile road trip with two other guys—one of whom doesn't "believe" in deodorant—isn't exactly all unicorns and rainbows.

I pushed my foot on the accelerator. The road stretched out before me, all the way to the horizon. Dark sand, dotted with cacti and shrubs, whipped by on either side. No sign of civilization for miles. Nature, untouched by man.

But then I saw it.

A shimmering light on the horizon. Shining like a beacon through the darkness.

And it was strange. As soon as the light met my eyes, I felt a wave of fatigue. It was like the Monster had worn off eight hours early. My arms ached, my fingers were stiff around the wheel, and my head felt so heavy...

"Actually, I think we should stop for the night," I said.

"What? You chickening out on us?" Dev asked.

"Fine with me," Emmett huffed.

The light twinkled and shimmered in the desert heat. I pushed down further on the accelerator, trying to reach it as fast as I could. *It's got to have a motel. Got to.* I glanced down, and noticed I was going near 80. I lay off a little.

"Might not be a motel," Dev said.

"Well, whatever it is, we're stopping. I at least need a coffee or something."

"Mixing coffee and Monster? That doesn't sound healthy, dude."

"I have a soy latte back here," Emmett offered, "if you want it."

I only made a gagging sound in reply.

The light on the horizon grew. Smaller lights appeared around it, and as we got closer, I could make out the details. A narrow road, shooting off from the highway and cutting into the sea of sand. Just a few buildings. I didn't see any huge, lit-up signs for motels—or even gas, or food—which did not bode well.

As I turned off on the exit, my heart dropped further. The off-ramp wasn't even marked with an exit sign—it was just... there. And the town itself...

No golden arches, no brightly-lit gas stations. The buildings that lined the street were all small, mom-and-pop type stores, that had long ago closed for the night. *Amy's Diner* read a sign overhanging a small brick building, the windows all foggy and gray. *Oak & Maple,* read another—as we passed, I could make out furniture, empty wooden chairs and dusty dressers.

"Sorry, bro," Dev said.

So tired...

I stifled a yawn as we approached the only intersection. The traffic light above us flashed yellow, bathing the closed shops in an eerie glow.

"Wait—there!" Dev said, excitedly. "Hotel!"

My eyes snapped up. He was right. There was a sign, small and inconspicuous, that simply read HOTEL with an arrow pointing left.

I swung left—and as soon as I did, the hotel came into view.

"Woah," Emmett said from the backseat.

It was fancy. Incongruous with the dark, run-down buildings we'd passed. Four stories stretched up to the starlit sky, the windows glowing softly gold. Victorian architecture, with turrets on either side, and curled embellishments under the gables. A sign stood in front, gold script on wood reading: **HOTEL ORA.**

"This is totally going to completely blow our budget," I said.

"You have to make sure they don't allow pets," Emmett piped up. "I'm very allergic to—"

"Oh my God, Emmett, please just shut up," Dev replied.

We pulled into the parking lot. Surprisingly, it was packed with cars. *But we're in the middle of nowhere*, I thought. *Who's sleeping here on a Sunday night, exactly? Lizards? Cowboys? Tumbleweeds?*

I pulled into the first empty space I saw. Then I stepped out of the car—and stopped.

The cars parked on either side of us... were *old*. One I recognized immediately—a Pontiac Firebird, from the '70s. The other I wasn't sure, but its chrome bumper and long hood seemed to be '70s or '80s as well. In comparison, my parents' 2012 Accord looked positively futuristic.

"Check it out! It's a Pontiac Firebird!"

"Cool," Dev replied. Emmett shrugged and started towards the front door of the hotel at a fast pace.

Lame. I took my phone out and snapped a photo of the Firebird. I'd never seen one in the flesh (or metal, as it were.) And as I put my phone back, I noticed something.

It looked... *new,* almost. The black paint was incredibly shiny, reflecting the streetlamps above us perfectly. Not a single chip or ding in its surface. The windows were clear, the seats inside were unblemished leather, and a pair of fuzzy dice hung from the rearview mirror.

"You gonna drool over that car all night?"

I turned to Dev. "Sorry, man," I said, breaking into a jog to catch up with him.

The three of us entered the lobby. It was beautiful—a two-story octagonal room, with dark oak walls and a chandelier. Hanging crystals diffracted the golden light in strange, broken shadows along the walls. A six-point buck stared at us from the back with glass eyes.

But the room was empty.

Emmett began ringing the bell on the counter as loudly as he could. Dev flopped onto one of the dark leather armchairs. My legs still felt like rubber from driving so long, so I paced around the room, examining the decorations.

Until I came upon the photos.

Three framed photos. Black-and-white, grainy. The

first showed a woman standing outside the hotel, smiling. The second, a guest standing in his room. The third, the same octagonal room we were standing in right now.

Boring. I was about to turn away—

And then I froze.

There was something... *off* about the photos. I leaned in to the first one, squinting. The woman standing out in front of the hotel wasn't smiling, exactly. When I got in close, I could see her lips stretched over her teeth in a pained grimace. And it was hard to tell with the low-quality photo, but I thought I could almost make out tears rolling down her cheeks.

What...?

I looked at the next photo. A man, standing in his hotel room. But... there was a thin line, above the man, breaking up the grainy shapes. *What is that?* I slowly traced its path down from the ceiling... to where it thickened and wrapped around the man's neck.

What the fuck—

"Matt."

I jumped.

"Come on," Dev said, clapping me on the back. "We got a room. Only 99 bucks. That's a steal for a place like this."

"But—" I turned back to the photos. But there was nothing wrong with them. The woman, she was smiling. The man, he was just standing in his room, no noose to be found. I rubbed my eyes, squinted, and stared at the grainy shades of gray.

"What?" Dev asked.

"Nothing," I muttered.

Man, I really did need some sleep.

I followed Dev through the doorway at the back of the room on shaky legs. Passed under the deer head and its glassy eyes. The hallway opened to a set of stairs, carpeted in a deep red rug with twisting, gold patterns.

"No elevator," Emmett said, as if reading my mind. "But we're only on the second floor."

We climbed the set of stairs and entered a dimly lit hallway. Too dimly lit, really, to be functional; the only light came from brass sconces between the doors, filled with a sort of fake firelight that flickered and danced. Old-style gold lettering was screwed to each closed door, but sometimes the letters hung slightly askew.

"Here we are," Emmett said. He reached into his pocket and pulled out—I kid you not—a *real* metal key. It slid into the lock with a satisfying *ching*, and then we were inside.

The room itself was nothing out of the ordinary. Small, with two beds set in white linen and a nightstand between them. A small bathroom sat off to the right, and thick red curtains hung over the only window. Out of curiosity, I walked over and peered out. Our room faced the hotel's courtyard area—not a true courtyard, as one side was open to the parking lot—and there was a nice little area with patio chairs and manicured shrubs. Even a fountain, water dripping softly from a concrete statue into a rectangular little pool.

Drip, drip, drip.

I sat down on the bed closer to the window with a

sigh. I pulled out my phone: 3:02 AM. Somehow I'd expected it to be a whole lot later than that.

"What's the WiFi password?" I asked.

"No WiFi," Dev replied.

"*What?!* No WiFi? No wonder it's only 99 dollars!"

Emmett rolled his eyes at me. "You know, it wouldn't hurt to be offline for five seconds. Read a book or something."

I raised an eyebrow at him. "I haven't read a book since high school."

"Engineers," he muttered.

"Come on, it's not so bad," Dev said, pulling the covers up to his chin. "Let's go to sleep, huh? That's what we came for, isn't it?"

"Okay, okay." I rolled away from Dev, and clicked out the light.

If only we knew what was going to happen that night, sleep would've been the last thing on our minds.

I woke up with a start.

For a second, I thought I was back in my dorm room. But then the unfamiliar gray shapes came into view, and the memories of the strange hotel flooded back. I glanced over to Dev—and froze.

The bed was empty.

I sat up. Looked over at Emmett's bed. His, too, was empty—the sheets all tangled in a lump, which was totally unlike him.

My feet hit the floor. I checked the bathroom, then swung the door open into the hallway. "Dev? Emm—"

"*Shhhh!*"

Dev grabbed my arm and pushed me back into the hotel room. As soon as I was inside, both of them rushed in behind me. Emmett slid the deadbolt. Dev panted like he'd just run a mile.

"What... are you guys doing?" I whispered.

"We got locked out—" Dev started.

"The power went out, so my white noise machine went off, and that always wakes—"

"Nobody fucking cares! Matt, there's someone out there." Dev stepped away from the door, glancing at it like someone might burst through at any moment. "We tried calling the front desk but the phones are out too. So we were going to the front desk and then we saw him. There is someone just *standing* there, in the middle of the fucking hallway, like a psychopath."

"Or... like another guest wanting to get to the front desk?" I offered.

Emmett snickered.

Dev crossed his arms. "Okay. Fine. You guys laugh." He crossed the room and began tossing his clothes into his bag. "I say we get the fuck out of here before whatever *that* is murders us."

I reached up to the deadbolt, then wrapped my hand around the doorknob. Before Dev could stop me, I pulled the door open—and stuck my head out into the hallway.

Dev was right.

There was a figure. Standing in the middle of the hallway, completely still.

Except it wasn't a psychopath—it was a woman.

An incredibly beautiful woman. Her face was illuminated only by the flickering candle in her hands. A soft, oval face with delicate features and dark eyes. Her blonde hair shone in the light, falling down her shoulders, nearly to her waist.

When she saw me, she smiled.

"You fucking idiot," I whisper-shouted back into the room. "You want to see what you were so afraid of?"

Dev looked at me with a blank expression.

I opened the door and stepped into the hallway. "Hey there," I said.

She was standing in the exact same place as I last saw her. But now, she was turned directly away from me.

"Your power's out, too?" I started, lamely.

She didn't reply.

I stepped towards her. The candlelight danced across the walls. Her hair blew, softly, glinting gold in the light. She was quite tall, and thin, wearing a white dress that reached the floor. A nightgown of some kind... though odd for her to just come out in that.

"Hey, are you okay?" I asked.

She slowly lifted her arm out in response—and curled her finger slowly, in a come-hither motion.

Huh. Curiosity piqued, I picked up my pace towards her. When I got within two steps of her, she started to slowly turn around.

I froze.

Every ounce of blood drained out of me.

She didn't have a face.

Blank skin stretched over the contours of her face. Over the sunken sockets where her eyes should be. Over the hollows of her cheeks, straight down to her chin, no mouth—

An arm grabbed me. Tight.

I screamed as Emmett dragged me back, faster than I thought he could run. In seconds I was on the floor of our room, still screaming like a baby, as the deadbolt clicked back into place.

A hand slapped my cheek. *Hard.* And then Dev's face appeared above mine.

"Be quiet, you fucking idiot. *They hear you.*"

And now, in the silence, I could hear it. Footsteps. Not just one set of them—many.

All getting louder.

"We'll go out the window. We're only on the second floor. No problem." But his voice shook as he spoke. "And then we drive as fast as we fucking can."

"Okay," I said.

My legs shook as I followed them over to the window. Emmett turned the lock, and with a grunt, slid the rusted window up. Dev reached over and pushed on the screen; it popped out of the window, falling onto the bushes below.

The footsteps were right outside the door.

"Go. *Go!*" Emmett whispered.

Dev wasted no time. He scooted out backwards, like he was climbing down an invisible ladder. He hung onto the ledge for a second, and then—*thud,* as his body hit the ground. "Fuck, that hurt," he whispered.

Emmett ran to the window next. He was significantly clumsier, contorting his tall frame to squeeze out the opening. He started to jump—

"*DON'T!*"

Dev's terrified yell met my ears.

His back was pressed against the wall. Features contorted in a look of terror that I had never seen on him before, as he stared into the hotel courtyard.

Where there was… a party?

Seconds ago, it'd been empty. But now there was a throng of people, dancing rhythmically to a melody played from unseen speakers. Red skirts twirled, black suits twisted, heels clicked along the gray flagstone with each dancing step.

And then I realized why Dev was so scared.

All together, they looked like a perfectly normal, dancing people. But when I focused on any one particular dancer… they were moving in a way no human possibly could. Their joints bending the wrong way. Their bodies twisting and contorting in a way that defied physics. Their heads swiveling too far around…

And they were, slowly, dancing towards Dev.

"I'm going to jump," Emmett said. "You right after, okay, Matt? And then we run for the car as fast as we can."

I nodded, my throat dry.

He gave me a nod—and then disappeared.

I climbed halfway through the opening, the window scraping my back. But as I stared down at them, my throat went dry. *That's a big drop.* Dev and Emmett, and all the dancers, looked so tiny. Like ants. Fear swept through my body. It felt like my blood had turned into a million tiny needles, pricking me inside, as I stared down at the dizzying distance—

"Matt! Jump!"

One of the dancers was only a few feet from them. A woman. Red dress. Dark hair flowing out behind her. Her neck bent at an unnatural angle. She twisted and contorted her body with the melody, her head flopping with each movement that made my stomach churn.

She's going to get them—

Jump. You have to jump.

I shut my eyes tight—and jumped.

Thud. Stinging pain shot through my chest. Gasping, I rolled over in the cold grass. Dev and Emmett grabbed my arms and forced me up. And as they did, I saw the woman's face up close.

It was the same woman from the photograph. The one who had been crying outside the hotel.

But this time, she was smiling.

"Run!"

The three of us ran across the grass. I could hear the rhythmic footsteps behind us, *feel* their eyes on us. But I didn't turn around. None of us did. We didn't stop until we were in the car, peeling out of the parking lot, coasting towards the highway.

After we graduated, we went our separate ways; Dev got a tech job in Seattle, I got a similar one in NYC, and Emmett is working on his PhD down south somewhere. None of us ever talk about what happened that night. If we do talk—which is rare these days—it's always just about work, or the 'good ol' days' during our first three years of college.

I'm glad they haven't brought it up. Because if they had, I might have told them.

That every night, before I drift off into sleep, I hear that strange melody from the courtyard. I see that beautiful blonde woman, standing in the corridor. I imagine driving that Pontiac Firebird down a dark desert highway.

No matter how many raises I get, no matter how wonderful my new girlfriend is, there is an emptiness. A void. An itch that can't be scratched, a hunger that can't be satiated. No matter what happens during the day, when my head hits the pillow, it's always that same melody playing in my head.

And if I really focus on it, I think I can make out four words, sung so softly they're almost inaudible.

You can never leave

SOMEONE IS LIVING IN MY FAIRY GARDEN

It started out as a fun project.

My daughter is obsessed with all things magical. Unicorns, fairies, everything. So I thought we could have fun building a fairy garden with her.

Boy, was I wrong.

We started in the west corner of the lawn, next to the vegetable garden. "This is their house, see?" I said, gesturing to a little stone cottage I'd bought at a flea market.

"Ooooh!" She was immediately hooked.

"And we can make them a path, out of these stones... and a little pond... and some moss for grass."

The whole project took two hours, but looked *amazing*. A cobblestone path, only two inches wide, wound up to the stone cottage. Mounds of moss sat on either side, mimicking tiny grass, and branches stuck in the ground were tiny trees. We'd even dug a small pond: a

6-inch-wide hole lined with aluminum foil we'd painted blue.

"Wow. I had no idea you were so crafty," my wife said, when we showed her.

"It's my little secret. So you won't ask me to help you redecorate the bathroom."

She stuck her tongue out at me.

"When will the fairies move in, Daddy?" Ava asked.

"Maybe tonight!"

"Can I leave them food? Maybe that will make them move in faster."

"Sure! How about some of Mommy's chocolate?"

Katie frowned at me.

" ...Just kidding. I think they'd love a pretzel."

That night, after Ava had gone to sleep, I went outside and took a bite of the pretzel. In the morning, we told her an elaborate story of how we'd heard them walking around at night. Little footsteps on the grass, hushed whispers, and tinkly laughter.

It's okay to lie to your kids about things that spark their imagination.

Right?

It was really Katie who took the whole thing to the next level. That evening, as dusk began to fall, I saw a light on in the fairy home. A soft white glow, coming from the upstairs window, reflecting in the tiny ripples of the pond.

Katie, you genius.

Ava was thrilled when she saw it. "Mommy! Daddy! The fairies have moved in!"

Katie smiled at me—a knowing smile. I winked back at her.

"Maybe they're like us. A fairy mommy, a fairy daddy, and a fairy girl!"

"Maybe they are."

"Can I meet them, Daddy? Pleeeaaase?"

I felt a twinge of guilt. Maybe it wasn't such a good idea to lie to Ava, after all. But Katie was quick on her feet.

"Fairies are allergic to people," she said, jumping in. "You know how you sneeze when you go over Samantha's house? Because you're allergic to her cat? Well, fairies are allergic to us. So if we go over there, we'll make them really sick."

Ava pouted. "Okay. I don't want to make them sick." Then her face lit up. "Maybe I can see them through the window! I'm going to stay up and watch them. All night."

Yikes.

"They already went to sleep," Katie replied. "And we need to go to sleep, soon, too."

"Why do they sleep with the light on?"

"They're afraid of the dark," I interjected.

"Oh."

After Ava fell asleep, we retreated to the bedroom. "That was brilliant. Putting a light in there."

Her brows furrowed. "I didn't put a light in there."

"What?"

"I thought you did."

My heart dropped. "You... you didn't put the light in there?"

She shook her head.

"But if you didn't, then who—"

Oh.

"It must have come with one. A solar-powered one. And it didn't charge up the first day." We'd had the same issue with the lights I got for the garden. They needed a full day to charge in the sun before turning on at night.

"And you only paid fifteen bucks, right? Pretty sweet."

"Yeah."

I stared out at the glowing light. Just a twinkle in the darkness—like a distant star.

I smiled and closed the curtains.

"Mommy! Daddy! I saw the fairies!"

Ava was bouncing up and down at the breakfast table, unable to contain her excitement.

"When did you see them?" Katie asked, not looking up as she poured syrup onto her plate.

"Last night! I woke up from a bad dream, and looked out the window, and they were out there!"

I shot Katie a look. "What... exactly... did you see?"

"Fairies!"

"What did they look like?"

"Fairies!"

Okay, this wasn't going anywhere. "What were they doing?"

"They were playing music and dancing! But then—then I think they saw me because they stopped dancing. I waved to them. They didn't wave back though." She frowned. "Maybe they're shy."

"She has such a big imagination," Katie said, as Ava ran to the window to look for them.

"I know. It's amazing."

Ava had always been imaginative. About a year ago, she made up two imaginary friends. Sentient horses that followed her everywhere. Whenever I asked what they were up to, she had some vivid description. *Diamond's balancing a ball on her nose right now! Hurricane's sneaking into the kitchen for an apple!*

Like she could *see* them.

"Daddy, Daddy, can we go outside?" she asked, tugging at my sleeve.

"Of course."

Ava spent most of the day playing outside, watching the fairy garden. She even dropped a goldfish cracker in the pond—"look, Daddy, the pond has fish now!"—and added a handwritten sign in front of the house.

It was around 4 pm that I noticed it.

I'd just sat down in the lawn chair with another iced coffee. But then I saw it: something pale and gray, barely poking up from the grass.

I got up and walked over, my heart beginning to pound. Crouched down, parted the grass.

It was a little mushroom.

Small and gray, popping up from the dark soil. A

circular cap fanning out from a thin stem, supported by dark brown gills.

"Ava, look. A mushroom!"

"Fairies LOVE mushrooms! They use them like chairs and umbrellas and all kinds of things!"

"... You know what, I bet they planted that mushroom on purpose."

And so, the fairy story continued.

Little did I know how terrifying it was about to get.

Snap.

I woke up with a start. Vivid dreams hung in my mind, of little people with wings and sharp teeth and tiny faces contorted into sneers. Dancing around their little home, then standing statue still as they noticed Ava watching them.

I looked at the clock. 3:42 AM. I rolled over, sighing—and froze.

A flurry of movement outside.

Someone in the yard. Walking towards the fairy garden.

Someone small...

"Ava. Oh, God, no." I jumped out of bed and raced down the stairs. Threw the backdoor open. "Ava! Come back in here!"

She didn't turn around.

I ran out into the yard, the grass cold and wet against my feet. "Ava!"

"Daddy," she said softly, not removing her gaze from the tiny stone cottage.

"When I'm calling to you—you *need* to listen." I joined her in front of the fairy garden, my heart hammering in my chest. "Why are you out here?"

"I wanted to see the fairies. They were dancing again."

"Ava, honey..." I swallowed, the guilt lead in my body. "There aren't any fairies. Okay? I'm so sorry. Mom and I made it up. This is just some stupid little house I bought at a flea market. And I ate the pretzel, not them. We've been... we've been lying to you, and it wasn't nice, and I'm sorry."

The door creaked open behind us as Katie walked out, still wearing her cat pajamas. She rushed over to us. "What's going on?"

"Ava was out here to see the fairies. And I... I told her they're not real."

She turned to me, slowly. "They are real, Daddy. I saw them."

"No. I don't know what you saw. But you didn't see fairies."

"But, Daddy—"

"I think we can talk about this in the morning," Katie said, forcing a smile. "Let's get back to bed, okay?"

She put her arm around Ava and led her back into the house. I just stood there, by the fairy garden, motionless.

Then I picked up the little cottage.

The stone exterior looked purple in the moonlight. The little door hung ajar. The two downstairs windows were dark, their tiny flowerboxes in shadow. But the upstairs window—a circular one hanging above the door—glowed white.

The glass was slightly frosted, but I could make out vague shapes inside. The artist had taken the time to create the illusion of a room. I squinted, trying to make out any details—

A dark shape flashed by the window.

I yelped and dropped the cottage. It bounced into the grass, rolled over the pond (which was now sludgy with goldfish crackers), and came to a stop inches from the mushroom. Face down, the windows pressed into the grass.

I didn't pick it up.

I ran into the house, slipping in the wet grass, my heart pounding in my chest.

A bug. A bug got caught into it. It must've been attracted to the light... and then couldn't find a way out.

That's what I told myself as I locked the door, clicked the deadbolt, and slipped back into bed.

Just a bug.

Katie and I sat across from each other, deep circles under our eyes, as Ava watched TV in the other room.

"We should've realized she'd go out there looking for them," Katie said, as she took a sip of tea.

"She's going to be so upset when I throw it out."

"Why don't we just bring it inside? Put it in her room, even. So she can check on the fairies anytime."

"Put the fairy cottage... in her room?"

Katie nodded.

My stomach twisted. "Uh... I guess we can bring it inside. But let's put it in the kitchen. If we put it in her room, she'll stay up all night."

"Good point."

I couldn't fight the unsettling feeling as I brought the cottage inside. The light in the upstairs window shone through the frosted glass. Bits of wet grass stuck to the stone exterior. I almost expected to feel movement inside—the scampering of little feet, panicking, as I relocated their home.

But of course, there was nothing.

Ava was so happy. "The fairies are with us now!" she kept saying, running over to the cottage and peering in the windows. "Do you think they like cookies?" She put one at their doorstep. "Or maybe cereal!"

The wet *plop* of soggy corn flakes hitting the table.

But the day went well, as we added little accessories to the indoor fairy home, went out to lunch, and played some board games.

It was that night that things went south.

Thump.

3:22 AM. I wasn't actually sure if I'd dreamed the noise or not, but I figured I'd better check on Ava. Yawning loudly, I pulled myself out of bed and shuffled down the hallway. But when I opened her door, I found her fast asleep, wrapped up in her unicorn blanket.

Good. I started back towards the bedroom—

Thump!

It wasn't a loud noise. Just a soft *thump*. Could

be the house settling, water rushing through the pipes and knocking in the walls. A badly-placed toy falling off a table, the fridge making ice. Still, my heart was pounding as I slowly descended the stairs.

"I'm calling 911," I called out—even though I'd left my phone upstairs.

I didn't expect a response. I truly didn't. I'd only said it in the tiny, fraction of a chance that someone had broken in and could hear.

But I did get a response. And it wasn't frantic footsteps to the door, or a getaway car revving its engine.

It was something far worse.

A giggle.

Coming from the kitchen.

Horror flooded me. "Who's there? Come out here where I can see you!"

I stepped through the living room. Taking a deep breath, I paused behind the wall—and then jumped out into the kitchen.

It was empty.

I stared at the only source of light in the kitchen. That one upstairs window of the fairy house, glowing like it always did. I stared at it without blinking. Wondering if I'd see that horrible little shadow flit by again.

Get a hold of yourself. There might be a real *person in the house, and you're looking for freaking fairies!*

I tore my eyes away from the cottage and scanned the kitchen. Empty. I poked my head out into the other doorway, where the kitchen connected with the dining room. Also empty. Everything was silent now, too, still as death.

I sucked in a deep breath and returned to the kitchen.

But something felt... different. A horrible sense of dissonance, unease. Like watching a happy scene in a horror movie, knowing the smiles and laughter are too much, and the killer's going to pop out any second.

I took a step towards the fairy home. Then another. And another. Tiny little faces flashed through my mind, their features contorted into horrific snarls, their eyes glowing unnatural yellow.

Get a hold of yourself.

I was standing right in front of the cottage now. Staring into that little white light.

There's. No. Such. Thing. As. Fairies.

I reached out and grabbed the fairy home. It felt strange in my hands—warm. Warmer than ceramic should be. I stared into that window, my heart thrumming in my chest.

And then it happened.

A flash of black, across the window.

It fell from my hands. I saw it in slow motion—the stone cottage careening to the ground, the jagged crack splitting it in two. The ceramic halves rolled away from each other. And from the innards—

Something flew out.

Something terrible and dark. It flew at my face and I screamed, swatting at it helplessly with my hands. I screamed again and then—

No.

It was a beetle.

Just an ordinary beetle, haplessly buzzing around the room, trying to find a way out.

Footsteps sounded above me now, as Katie rushed out of bed. As Ava began to cry. "Oh, Ava, I'm so sorry." I looked down at the remains of the fairy house, hopelessly destroyed.

Wait...

What... is that?

I crouched to the ground. Nestled inside the ceramic was something small, shiny, white. I reached over and picked it up. The smooth surface was warm against my hands—almost hot. I turned it over.

Then I realized what it was.

A camera.

With a microphone, a speaker... and a little white light glowing on it.

Showing it was recording.

I WAS INVITED TO A SWINGER'S PARTY

"Uh, Marlene," I started, my throat dry. "I don't know how to tell you this. But just before I left O'Neill's... this woman came up to me. And she, uh, invited me to an orgy."

Marlene stared at me.

And then she burst out laughing. "A woman... came up to *you*... and invited you to her orgy," she repeated, through giggles.

"Technically she called it a *swinger's party*, but yeah." My frown deepened. "Is that really so hard to believe?"

"Well, yeah, kinda." Her smile faded. "Oh, no, that's not what I meant. You know I think you're sexy as hell."

"Yeah, yeah," I said, smirking at her. "Anyway, of course, I said no. But I just wanted to tell you, because I don't want some sort of situation to come up where I tell Sam, and Sam tells you, and you think I..."

"Let's go to it."

"*What?*"

"Not like *that*," she said quickly. "Look. My last few articles haven't gained any traction. I don't think they're going to renew my contract." She shook her head. "Can you imagine what a post that would make? *What Swinger's Parties are Like in 2022*. I bet I'd break a hundred thousand views."

I stared at her, chewing my lip.

"Don't worry! We won't *do* anything. As soon as clothes start coming off and things start getting freaky, we'll leave. But I could write a whole thing on it. What's it like? Is it in a basement sex dungeon or a high-class hotel? Are the people super-hot or weird? What's the small talk like?"

"I don't think there *is* any small talk."

"See? That's exactly what we need to find out! Is there small talk? Are there hors d'oervres shaped like—"

"I don't think this is a good idea."

"Oh, come on, why not?"

"ISN'T IT OBVIOUS?!"

"Look. It's easy. We show up. As soon as it starts, you pretend to get a phone call. Oh my God, your brother's in the hospital! You have to go. Too bad, you were so excited for this. We run out the door and drive away."

I sighed. "I see what you're saying, but... no. I'm not going. Absolutely not."

"I can't believe you talked me into this."

Marlene grinned at me from the passenger seat. She'd gotten dressed up for the thing, bobby pins in her wild hair and glittery eyeshadow on her lids. "Aren't you *excited?*"

"No."

She punched me in the arm. "Lighten up a little."

I only frowned, staring at the road ahead.

The woman sounded pretty excited when I called and said we were coming—which, I gotta admit, was an ego boost for me. She told me she had to "vet" me first, and asked me a series of questions, ranging from *"Are you open to BDSM?"* to *"What is your blood type?"*.

Then she gave me the address and time.

The location was way out of town. We'd been driving for twenty minutes now, and each turn we made led us on a narrower and narrower road. Suburban houses morphed into deep woods, picket fences into dense fog. The road we were currently on, Cedar Road, twisted and curved up a hill, probing deeper into the thick forest.

"We drove out into the middle of Bumblefuck, Nowhere," Marlene said as she pressed the record button on her phone. *"I guess that makes sense. This party will probably be loud. Like, really loud. Dan said there are going to be more than forty people..."*

"Taking notes, I see," I replied, as I swung onto an even narrower road.

"Yep. Hey, can you slow down? I want to take a photo."

I obliged. Marlene rolled down her window and then stuck her phone out, taking a photo of the narrow road and the woods on either side.

"*Your destination will be on the right in 50 feet,*" my phone's GPS interrupted.

And then I saw it: the entrance to a driveway. At its base, nailed to the trunk of a large oak tree was a bronze "1". I pulled in.

The driveway, only wide enough for one car, snaked through the forest. And through the trees, further up the hill, a mass of golden lights glimmered.

"*The orgy's in a fucking mansion!*" Marlene said gleefully into her phone.

Several cars were lined up on the grass beside the three-car garage. We parked at the far end, next to a shiny Mercedes SUV. As we walked up to the front door, I couldn't help but stare at the place. Elegant gray stone, enormous windows, and a gabled roof that seemed to go on forever.

Marlene rang the doorbell—and the door promptly swung open to reveal a woman.

I don't know what I was expecting, but it certainly wasn't *her*. She was tall and bone-thin, in her late thirties or early forties, wearing head-to-toe black clothing. Not dominatrix-style, not leather or lace, just a simple black shirt and pants.

And I think she was wearing a wig.

"Please, come inside," she said, a small smile curling on her lips.

We stepped into a grand foyer, the ceiling yawning above us, a crystal chandelier lit with dim electric lights. But except for our own footsteps, the mansion was silent. "I'll take your coats," the woman said, pinning a lock of plasticky-blonde hair behind her ear.

As soon as she disappeared, Marlene pulled out her phone.

"We are greeted by a woman when we come in," she whispered. *"Wig, black clothing, weird eyeliner. Sort of a discount Lady Gaga type."*

"Sssshhh!" I said, stifling a laugh.

"Oh, and Dan thinks I'm the hottest woman here."

"That's true."

"However, there are only two women so far. Me and Discount Gaga. Where is everyone? Clearly all the sexy sex is happening upstairs, or downstairs, or somewhere that is not here. We are standing alone in a completely silent mansion. Cool."

Clicking footsteps on the wood. Marlene quickly pocketed her phone as the woman returned out of the darkness. She gave us another smile—a smile that didn't quite reach her eyes.

Then she motioned for us to follow her.

Marlene gave me an eyebrow waggle—and then followed.

She led us from the foyer into a dimly-lit hallway. For such a big house, it felt narrow. My shoulders were nearly bumping the walls.

And that's when I saw them.

The decorations.

A traditional African mask hung on the wall, white markings surrounding empty eye sockets. Then an Egyptian painting—a bloody heart weighed against a feather, as Anubis watched. I guess they were the decorations I'd expect from some world-traveling millionaire. Artifacts stolen from other cultures to show how "cultured" they were.

And yet... looking at them sent chills up my spine.

I poked Marlene's elbow, nodding to the various items. Her face lit up. Glancing at the woman, she slipped out her phone out and took a photo of another mask. This one was from a culture I didn't recognize, with blood-red markings and a mouth twisted into a snarl.

"The house has creepy decorations. Oooooooooo."

I forced a smile. But inside, my heart was starting to pound. *Where is everyone?* The mansion was still as death, even as we walked further into its depths. *This could totally be a trap. The woman I met at the bar was a stranger. She could be an axe-murderer, for all I knew.*

An axe-murderer who, for some reason, targets balding history professors?

Okay. It didn't make much sense, when I thought about it. But still. My heart pounded faster as my eyes fell on a Greek vase, depicting two men stabbing each other. A shard of terracotta pottery with indents in it that almost looked like teeth marks. A scroll of papyrus covered in hieroglyphics, that grew more and more frantic towards the bottom, as if the writer was rushing to get the words out as fast as he possibly could—

I bumped into Marlene.

"Can't wait until the main event?" she shot back at me, grinning.

I stepped away from her. "Sorry. I didn't see that we'd stopped..."

The woman was standing in front of a door. She

swung it open—and as soon as she did, noise met our ears. Laughter. Conversation. The *clink* of drinking glasses and silverware.

Relief flooded me.

"Everyone's downstairs," the woman said, smiling.

Now, in the bright white light of the basement stairwell, Discount Gaga didn't look so creepy either. I could see a tangle in her plastic wig-hair, a smudge of eyeliner. She probably just wore the wig to protect her identity. It's not like you want someone recognizing you at the grocery store and saying *hey, I remember you from the orgy last week!*

"Thank you," Marlene said, offering the woman a warm smile.

I gave her a nod and a smile, feeling bad that I'd misjudged the whole thing.

We stepped onto the stairwell—

And the door slammed shut behind us.

"Uh, okay, that was weird..." I reached behind me and grabbed the doorknob. Turned it. It was locked.

I turned it back and forth, jiggling it with all my strength. *Click, click, click.* Marlene's brown eyes widened.

"Maybe... this is part of it? Part of the sex game?"

"I don't like this." She pulled out her phone, and convincingly said into it: "Hello? ... Are you kidding? ... Oh my God, that's horrible! Is he okay? – Hey, I'm so sorry everyone, but my brother got in a car accident. We have to go."

No response—from either the woman on the other side of the door, or the people below.

"Hey! Did you hear me? We. Have. To. Go."

No response.

I turned and slapped my hand on the door. "Hey! We want to leave. Let us out!"

Silence.

And then I realized...

The sound downstairs had stopped. No conversation, no laughter, no *clinking* of dinnerware.

Marlene and I stared at each other, wide-eyed.

"What the fu—"

The lights flickered—and then cut out.

We were plummeted into darkness. And then pain shot through me, as Marlene grabbed my arm. Her fingernails dug into me as she pulled me close. "We have to get out of here."

"I don't—we're locked in—"

Click.

The softest sound. From below us. A high heel clicking on wood, as though the person was trying to be as quiet as possible.

"Hey, I don't know what kind of fucked-up roleplay this is," Marlene shouted at whoever was watching us. "But we do *not* consent to this. Let us out."

A few soft thumps below. Others joining her. I could picture them, all swarming around the foot of the stairs. Watching. Waiting.

They knew we were trapped.

It was just a matter of time.

Marlene was crying. I could hear her shaking breaths as her fingernails dug into me. I wrapped an arm around her—but I didn't know what to do. *Go up,* and the door's locked. Go down, and... how many are down there, waiting for us?

Ten? Twenty? Fifty?

We were outnumbered.

"What do you want? Money?" I reached into my pocket, pulled out my wallet. "Here. Take it. A hundred bucks. Take the cards too. Just, please, let us out."

I threw it down the stairs. I heard it thud somewhere at the bottom, a split-second later. Followed by... silence. No thumps, no rustling of clothes.

No one was picking it up.

They don't want money. My heart dropped further. *Of course they don't want money. This is a fucking mansion. But then... what do they want? Sex? Is this really only about sex?*

My hands were cold. A horrible, prickly feeling coursed over my skin. Nothing made sense—and that was terrifying. *What possible reason could they have to trap two middle-aged, middle class people in their basement?*

As if to answer my question, a candle flickered on.

Orange light danced off the walls. Marlene's terrified face was thrown into relief, her tears glinting on her cheeks. I looked down—and saw a dozen figures below us, standing frozen at the bottom of the stairs.

Black robes covered their bodies. Hoods hung over their faces, hiding them in shadow. The flame continued to dance, giving the illusion of movement.

And then they began to chant.

Low and guttural. A language I didn't recognize. It sounded strange on their tongues—like human mouths were never meant to utter them.

One of them took a step up the stairs.

Marlene squeezed my arm so hard I yelped. The chants grew in volume as another robed person followed them, then another. *We're trapped. There's no way out. How do we—*

Marlene pulled a bobby pin out of her hair. Frantically, she shoved it into the tiny hole in the doorknob. *Click, click...* "come on, come on," she whispered shakily.

Several of them were on the stairs now. Faces hidden. Chanting in those low, guttural tones.

Click, click... POP.

Marlene pushed the door open.

The woman was still there. She rushed at us as we pushed through the opening. Marlene shot down the hallway as the woman grabbed my arm, desperately trying to pull me back. I yanked and tilted, and her fingers slipped.

I sprinted after Marlene.

The chants echoed behind us as we ran down the hallway. The Greek vase, the Egyptian artwork, the African masks—they all stared at us with hollow eyes as we scrambled through, bursting into the foyer and tearing out the front door.

As we peeled out of the driveway, I could see them in the rearview mirror. Standing in the doorway. Watching us leave. They had taken down their hoods—and the horror of it is, they all looked like ordinary people. All races, all genders, ranging from twenty to seventy. Pretty, ugly, short, tall, just an average group of people you'd see on the street.

And their lips were still moving.

We called the police, but by the time they got to the mansion, it had been cleared out. Nothing remained but our jackets, which we collected from the police station after giving our statements. "A cult looking for human sacrifice" was the prevailing opinion of what happened to us. Apparently, the police had received other reports of cult activity in the area.

Marlene didn't write the article, for fear that the cult—or whatever they were—would find us and retaliate. She did, however, keep her notes and photos on her phone. "Maybe someday I'll write it," she said to me, sadly. "When they're caught and can't hurt us anymore."

One night, a few weeks after the incident, she called me over to the couch. "Hey, uh, Dan," she said, "can you come take a look at this?"

One look at her face told me this was serious. Confused, I sat down next to her.

Without a word, she pulled out her coat—the coat she had brought the party. She pulled it open, showing me the lining of the collar. Then she slipped her fingers inside a small hole, where the lining met the coat.

She pulled out a small piece of wood, carved with jagged symbols.

"They left this in my coat," she said, her voice shaking. "I've been wearing this coat every day. Every. Single. Day."

She reached into the pockets of the coat. Pulled out

wads of tissues, stained red. She looked at me, then began to sob.

"I—I've been coughing up blood. For two days. I think... I think they knew we were going to escape," she said, her voice breaking. "And I'm still their sacrifice."

MY NEIGHBOR'S BACKYARD

"What the hell are they building?"

It was almost nine PM, but the loud *clangs* from the Robertsons' backyard could be heard loud and clear.

Nate shrugged. "Adding onto their deck, maybe?"

It was a shame the Robertsons had that fence. Six and a half feet of premium cedar and absolutely spy-proof. Otherwise I could get a look—and maybe tell them to keep it down, too.

"They better stop by 10. I'm dead tired."

Clang. Clang. Scccrrrrape.

"I'm going to take on more overtime so we can move to a 10 acre farm in the middle of nowhere."

"Sounds good to me," he replied, munching on another chip.

I had to admit, it was a little odd. The Robertsons were a childless couple in their 70s. They spent most of their time indoors. Sometimes I'd see Adelaide tending to her flowers out front, or hear Greg talking on the back deck, but that was really it.

What could they possibly be building?

It wasn't small. I could tell that much, by the reverberating *clangs* and heavy *thumps*. Large pieces of *something* were being moved around their backyard, assembled by the occasional *whirr* of a power tool.

"Hey. Let's bet on it. I bet they're building... one of those fancy light-up jacuzzis," Nate said, folding up the chip bag. "Where you can see *everything*."

"Eugh, Nate. They're so *old!*"

"So what? They don't deserve a fancy jacuzzi? That's very ageist of you." He laughed and folded up the chip bag. "So. What do you bet?"

"I'll go with the deck idea."

"Okay. Winner picks the next date night."

He reached out his hand, and I shook it.

Two days later, the sounds had not ceased.

Clang. Scrape. Whirr. You could hear it every day, from about noon to ten pm. But it always seemed louder at night. More frantic.

"I think we should go over and talk to them," I whispered to Nate, as we sat on the back deck. "How long is this going on for? A week? A month?"

"I dunno if that's a good idea, Maggie."

"I wasn't going to say anything rude. Just... you know... ask them some questions."

I stared out into our backyard, deep blue in the dusk. I'd really tried to make it nice for summer—to turn it into one of those spaces you see on catalogs and Pinterest. A mirror ball, a wind spinner, flowers...

But it was a failure. First, the horrible noises next door. But also... the mirror ball cracked after Paprika knocked it over, the wind spinner squeaked when it spun, and the petunias all died. I knew next to nothing about gardening, and a week after planting they turned brown, flopping over into the grass.

"I'm going back inside," he said, standing. "These mosquitos are crazy."

Oh. And the mosquitos. How could I forget those?

I sighed, staring out at my twelve-hundred square-foot failure. "I think I'll stay out for a few more minutes."

After he disappeared, I walked over to the fence. The eerie blue glow glinted off the leaves of our crepe myrtle, danced across the overhanging branches of the forest beyond. I crept right up to the cedar fence and stretched as tall as I could on tiptoe. Not tall enough. I paced along it, looking for a crack or knot in the wood I could peer through. Nothing.

A shadow passed over the blue glow, briefly throwing the branches back into darkness. And then the sound started up again: *clang, clang, clang.* Loud and frantic.

Paprika's barks sounded inside the house a moment later. Also loud and frantic.

That's it.

With a glance at the window to make sure Nate

wasn't watching, I snuck around the side and marched over to the Robertsons'.

It took a full minute for someone to come to the door. Then it cracked open, and Greg Robertson poked his head out.

He looked terrible. Dark circles under his eyes. Beads of sweat on his forehead. His button-up shirt wrinkled, a faint brown stain on the sleeve.

"Yes?"

My confidence deflated a little. "Sorry to bother you. But the construction you're doing in the backyard... it's really bothering our dog. Do you think you could try to stop the noise a little earlier in the evening?"

"I'm sorry. Of course, I'll try."

He kept his voice soft, almost a whisper. I wondered if his wife, Adelaide, was sleeping—but then I noticed her form beyond him. Sitting at the kitchen table with a cup of tea, her back to us, staring out into the backyard.

The backyard.

I squinted at the eerie blue glow that shone beyond the deck, trying to make out—

"I have to be somewhere," Greg said abruptly.

And then he slammed the door in my face.

The construction went late into the night.

Nate slept right through it. He's a deep sleeper.

Someone could be playing death metal full blast next door and he wouldn't wake up.

Me, on the other hand...

Yawning, I got up and stared out the window.

All the houses in our neighborhood are one-level, so I still couldn't see into his backyard. I could only see that strange bluish glow, shining on the overhanging leaves that danced in the breeze.

Clang. Crash. The sounds throbbed in my ears. I glanced at the nightstand clock—12:42 AM.

This is ridiculous.

I put on a robe and charged downstairs—then ran over to the fence.

"Hey! It's almost 1 AM! Can you *please* stop?!"

Surprisingly—the sounds stopped.

Silence.

But *total* silence. No Greg or Adelaide calling back to me. No thuds of footsteps or dropping tools.

The hairs on the back of my neck prickled. I froze, an unsettling feeling forming in my gut. Something felt... off. Slowly, I turned around.

The kitchen light was on.

The blinds were pulled down, but I could see vague shapes through the cracks. The granite island. The yellow incandescent lights. The kitchen table—and Adelaide, sitting at it.

Still staring into the backyard.

A chill went down my spine. I backed into the house, closed the door, and slid the deadbolt.

By the time I made it upstairs, the *clanging* had resumed. Peering out through the blinds, I watched the shadow shift across the branches as Greg—or whoever it was—continued their work.

They worked well into the night. My sleep was horrible, a series of disjointed dreams. And the noise wasn't just clanging and whirring—I thought I heard other stuff, too. Clicking, like a dysfunctional telephone line. Buzzing, which inspired a nightmare about gigantic bees.

But I think they were finally done.

When I got back from work, it was totally quiet. Not a single *clang*. I went out into the backyard, sat in one of our chairs, and breathed in the fresh air. *Maybe we'll turn this thing into a dreamy Pinterest space, after all.* Inspired, I turned on the hose and watered my dead petunias until the backyard looked like it had flooded.

"I guess they're done with whatever they were building, huh?" Nate asked, as he joined me outside.

"I think so," I replied, turning off the hose.

I hadn't told him about either of my interactions with the Robertsons last night. I knew he'd just criticize me for "starting trouble" with the neighbors. Even though, clearly, *they* were the ones starting trouble first.

He walked along the fence. "I can't see a thing. How are we going to know who won the bet? I guess I'll have to hoist you up and throw you over!"

I frowned.

"Wait, wait. I think I hear something!" He broke into a grin. "Oh man, it really *is* a jacuzzi!"

I joined him by the fence. Put my ear to the cedar. And then I heard it.

A soft, wet gurgling sound.

"Could be a fountain, on their *new deck*," I said, with a smirk.

"You're grasping at straws."

"There's only one way to find out. Let's get the ladder—"

Arf!

We both snapped around. Paprika was on the deck, staring at us. Growling, low and steady, ears pinned back.

"Paprika, what's wrong?"

Arf!

It took almost an hour for Paprika to calm down. Only when we brought her inside and fed her half a dozen treats did she settle down quietly on her doggie bed. And by that time, we'd forgotten all about settling the bet.

That night, I fell asleep early, happy to finally have peace and quiet.

I woke up early the next morning, refreshed after a deep and uninterrupted sleep. While Nate showered, I walked out into the backyard with my cup of coffee, enjoying the cool summer morning and the peaceful silence.

I was halfway through my cup when I saw it.

My petunias.

Thick green leaves curled out from healthy stems. Deep purple petals glowed more vivid than ever. I crouched down and touched one of the leaves—silky soft.

"Well, I'll be damned. All you guys needed was a little water, huh?"

Their velvety petals glowed back at me.

I went back inside and set my coffee cup in the sink. Then I walked over to Paprika, who was sitting in her dog bed. "Hey, girl. Time to go out."

She whimpered and buried her head under one of the little pillows.

"Really?"

Paprika *always* needs to go out in the morning. I frowned and crouched over her, patting her shoulder. "Hey, you don't want to go out?"

Another whimper.

Nate's heavy footsteps sounded on the stairs. "Paprika doesn't want to go outside," I called. "I'm worried."

"You think something's wrong?" He crouched next to me. "Hey, girl, don't you need to go out?"

She whined again.

Nate eventually tricked her outside with a treat, but she stayed as far as she possibly could from the Robertsons' fence as she went to the bathroom. I finished my breakfast, fixed up my makeup a little, and then headed out to the driveway.

And there was Adelaide.

She was hunched over the flowerbeds in front of their house, intently working the soil. Wearing her usual outfit of black flats and a floral dress, with large, splotchy watercolor roses across the back.

"Hi, Adelaide!"

She didn't reply.

Didn't even turn around.

I stood there for a second, waiting. For her to wave, stand, or at least acknowledge my presence *somehow*. She didn't. Just kept working on those flowers as if I weren't even there.

How rude. I settled into the driver's seat, scowling. *If anything, I should be the one mad at* them *for making so much noise all night.*

As I pulled out of the driveway, I couldn't help but notice the Robertsons' flowers looked especially healthy that morning.

"And she wouldn't even say hi."

I scrubbed furiously at the dish in my hand, scraping at the dried bits of cheese that held on for dear life. "*They* were the ones making all kinds of noise. All *I* did was ask them to not do it so late at night."

"You went over there?"

"Yeah, I did," I said, sliding the dish into the upper rack. "And you shouldn't be so disapproving. I was barely getting any sleep. Paprika was a nervous wreck. There are laws about disturbing the peace, you know."

Nate didn't say anything. Just pressed his lips into a thin line.

"Come on, Nate. Don't be ridiculous."

"I'm not being ridiculous. You're the one yelling."

"I'm not yelling."

We did the rest of the dishes in silence. Paprika happily chewed on her bone, the TV mumbled softly in the background. Dark clouds gathered overhead, heavy with impending rain. Thunder rumbled in the distance.

"Storm's coming," Nate said. "I'm going to bring in the chairs."

I sat down at the kitchen table with a box of cookies as he walked into the darkening shadows of our backyard. I watched as he picked up one of the upholstered chairs, paused... and started towards the Robertsons' fence.

The curiosity lit in me like a spark.

I ran out to meet him. Grabbed the second chair and dragged it towards the fence. "So we're going to settle this now, huh?"

"Yep."

Small drops of rain fell, pattering on the bright green grass. Grass that, I realized, was much greener on this side of the backyard.

"If I win, I'm taking you to that couple's cooking class," I said, stepping up onto the seat. "We're gonna make *pan-seared salmon.*"

He recoiled. "You wouldn't."

"Oh, I would."

"If *I* win, then, I'm taking you to my book club." He leaned in close. "And you have to read the book before we go."

"Noooooooo!"

"Okay," Nate said, climbing up onto the chair. "On the count of three. One... two..."

We hoisted ourselves up onto the chairs.

And peered into the Robertsons' backyard.

What... is that?

It wasn't a jacuzzi or a deck. It was something I didn't recognize. An oblong metal container, with no markings on it. Something about its shape—wider on one end, with curved edges—reminded me of a coffin. A dozen thin tubes connected to it, with bubbling dark liquid inside. Wires from multiple points on the "coffin" met in the center of the backyard, twisting together to form a multicolored snake of wires that ran back to the house. A high-pitched mechanical whine cut through the distant thunder.

"What *is* that?" I whispered.

"I don't know."

"It looks like it's from a sci-fi movie or something."

"Isn't Greg an engineer? Maybe he invented something," Nate replied. "Maybe he's going to get a patent and become rich and famous and—"

A low *thump* cut him off.

Greg Robertson stood inside the kitchen. He looked worse than last time, heavy circles under his eyes, his face pale and gaunt. But one thing was for certain—he was watching us.

And he looked *angry*.

Nate and I ducked behind the fence. "He saw us, he saw us," I whispered.

"So? We were just looking."

But something about Greg's expression shot fear through me. I grabbed Nate's hand and pulled him towards the house.

The rain was pelting down, now, in heavy sheets that made the grass slick under our feet. But I didn't stop running, didn't let go. We burst inside, and slid the door as hard as I could, clicked the lock.

"We didn't do anything wrong, Maggie."

"He looked *so* angry," I replied, pulling the blinds across the glass. "Do you think whatever that thing is... it's illegal?"

Nate paused. "You think he's making drugs with that thing?"

I thought of the dark liquid I'd seen, bubbling through the tubes. "No. I don't think so. But he's—"

Thunk-thunk-thunk!

"He's at the door," I whispered.

"Don't answer it," Nate replied.

Paprika was frozen in her dog bed. Ears pinned back, teeth bared. But she wasn't barking. Wasn't making a single sound.

I'd never seen her so terrified.

Thunk-thunk-thunk! Louder this time. Faster. Light flashed outside, followed by a peal of thunder.

"We can't—"

Nate wrapped his arms around me. "Ssshh. He'll can't stay there forever. Just... wait." Paprika stared at us, eyes wide.

I turned to the front door, to the window next to it. The blinds were closed, but I could see a sliver of Greg's arm, raised up to knock again.

An arm clad in colorful florals...

"It's not Greg," I whispered. "It's Adelaide."

Thunk-thunk-thunk! The door shook on its hinges with incredible force.

More force than a short, frail, seventy-year-old woman could muster.

And then a thought flashed through my mind. That day I'd seen her, tending to the flower beds... I thought those were large, splotchy roses painted across the back. But now I realized, they didn't fit with the tiny blue flowers on the rest of her dress...

And they were the color of dried blood.

Lightning flashed, illuminating Adelaide's silhouette through the curtains. A silhouette that was slightly twisted, contorted, *off.* Her arm moved in a strange, jerky motion as she raised it to the door.

Thunk-thunk-thunk.

WHY WE'LL NEVER GO TO MARS

I know why we'll never go to Mars.

It's because we've already been there.

I can't tell you who I work for. Let's just say, it's a prominent tech company that has built space exploration vehicles.

I'm not an astronaut, or even an engineer. I work in the records department. My job is really boring: I digitize old files. Not files about space or astronauts or the secrets of the universe. Just old patent applications, interoffice complaints... that kind of thing.

That all changed when I was assigned to the Andromeda records.

I think they gave it to me by accident. All the stuff I've worked on has been in the records room, but these were in a locked closet of the sub-basement. When I walked in, everything was coated in a thick film of dust. "Yay, allergies," I muttered, grabbing one of the boxes and hauling it back to the elevator.

The first folder contained extensive background checks on three people: George Thomas, Jayne Kowalski, and Alex Chang. It had their photos, too. George Thomas was quite handsome, with deep brown skin and upslanting eyes. Jayne Kowalski was thin and willowy, with a gaunt face and high cheekbones. Alex Chang seemed a little bit older than the other two—his temples were gray, and deep laugh lines sat in the corners of his eyes.

I fed them into the scanner while watching some TikTok video of a guy making homemade ramen cups.

The next folder had photographs. About a dozen of them. I pulled them out one-by-one and lay them on the desk. They looked like photos of the Nevada desert; orangey sand and rocks stretching as far as the eye could see. Faded mountains in the background.

I fed them into the scanner too.

The next folder, though, didn't have any paper in it. It had a cassette, like the ones I listened to music on as a kid. It wasn't unusual to find CDs or USB sticks mixed in with the files--this place was disorganized as fuck. But I'd never found a cassette before. I scrounged up a player from the storage closet.

Then I fed it in and hit PLAY.

"It is March 2nd, 1993," a man's voice said through the speakers, slightly distorted. "This is the crew of the Andromeda Two speaking—myself, Captain George Thomas, Alex Chang, and Jayne Kowalski. And in seven short months... we will be the first people to ever set foot on Mars."

I froze. Rewound the tape.

Played it again.

I glanced around the office. No one was paying attention. Of course—I was wearing headphones.

"It's incredible, looking down at the Earth from up here. Every single person you've ever loved, every thing we've ever made, the entire history of humanity is contained in that little blue sphere. Except for us."

"I think you missed your calling as a poet," a male voice joked—presumably Alex.

"Oh, let me have my fun. There's not much else to do in this tiny ship."

"You should write a book," Jayne said, her voice tinged with a slight Slavic accent. "I bet it would sell very well. 'The Book I Wrote In Space.' And the cover could be—"

I pressed the fast forward button. Garbled, high pitched sound as the wheels spun.

"April 17th, 1993. Alex bested the three of us in an on-board chess tournament. We've—"

I held down fast forward. When it got to the end of the tape, I flipped it over and fast-forwarded until I got close to landing day.

"October 21st, 1993. We are landing in just four days. We can see Mars pretty well from here. An orange sphere, painted in shades of the sunset, hanging in the black void of space." Despite the poetic description, the Captain's voice sounded tired.

"Can you turn up the heat?" Jayne asked, her voice distant. Or maybe she was just talking quietly.

A pause. "Sure, I'll turn it up, Jayne."

"October 22nd, 1993. Just three more days until we

land. I can't believe we are going to be the first people to step foot on Mars. How are we doing, crew?"

"Excited," Alex's voice replied.

"A little nervous," followed Jayne's.

"October 23rd, 1993. We land the day after tomorrow. We thought we hit a snag with Deimos's orbit, but we've been given the all clear. On our first day on Mars, we'll—"

"Hey, Captain? Where's the Dramamine being kept?"

"Should be in the med drawer. Why, you sick?"

"Jayne's throwing up a bit."

"Sorry to hear that."

"October 24th, 1993. We land tomorrow. Mission control just informed us that there's been some technical glitching going on—about 5% of our messages aren't going through. It shouldn't affect the landing, as everything is on autopilot at this stage. But we'll need to improve the communications devices for next time."

"October 25th, 1993. We're here. I can't believe it." George's voice came through, loud and clear. "We're going to be the first three people on Mars."

"Do you have your line ready, Captain? *One giant leap for mankind?*" Alex asked.

"No, haven't got a damn thing. But it isn't televised, so it doesn't matter." A few mechanical *clicks* and *clangs*. "Now, come on, crew. Let's get those suits on."

Rustling and thumping sounds went on for several minutes. Then, finally, the Captain's voice came back on.

"It is October 25th, 1993. I am standing here with

my crewmates, Alex Chang and Jayne Kowalski. And the three of us are about to walk where no man has ever walked before."

A loud *th-thunk*. Then a low *creeeeak*. I could picture it in my head—something out of a sci-fi movie. A door opening upwards, revealing a vast expanse of red desert. The gray mountains rising up in the distance. The sun beating down, lighting the alien terrain—

"Close the door."

Jayne's voice. Low and fearful.

"What's wrong?" Alex's voice.

"Close the fucking door!"

"Jayne—"

Thumping sounds. I could hear Jayne's voice, crying, whimpering. The creak and *th-thunk* of the door being closed. I waited, my heart thrumming in my chest.

There was a *click* as the recorder was shut off. A beat of silence.

And then George's voice.

"October 26th, 1993." His tone was sobered—and he was speaking quietly, as if he didn't want to be heard. "Jayne's condition is... not improving. She stays in her bunk all day, hiding under the blankets. Sometimes I hear her muttering, but I don't know what she's saying because it's all in Polish. I described it to mission control, and the psychiatrist consult said it's PSRD. Post Seclusion Reaction Disorder, I think, is what it stands for. She's mentally breaking down after being confined in space for seven months."

He lowered his voice further, nearly whispering.

"I don't know, though. Why now? Why not break

down two months ago? Why break down at the *exact moment* we opened the door? I'm not a psychiatrist, but... that doesn't make sense."

He blew out a breath.

"And, God, the look in Jayne's eyes. They're just blank. I don't think I've ever seen someone—"

"Hey, what are you doing?" Alex's voice, from a distance.

"Nothing. Just recording to the Captain's Log." A rustling sound. "Do you need something?"

"I wanted to talk to you. I think we should go out, tomorrow... without Jayne."

"Mission control said she could recover in a few days."

"Yeah, 'could.'" Alex's voice gained a sharp edge. "We've already lost an entire day, George. Our take-off day is fixed. You know that."

"But Jayne..."

"We'll leave her in the ship, safe and sound. Maybe in a few days she'll be better, and then she can join us."

A long pause. A sigh. A creaking sound.

"Okay, I'll think about it."

Click. The recorder shut off. A few seconds of silence. And then—

"She went without us."

There was no preamble, no stating the date. Just George's shaking voice as he talked into the recorder.

"Her suit is missing. Footprints leading away from the ship." He let out a shaking breath. *"Dammit."*

Alex's voice cut in, his tone bitter. "I bet it was on

purpose. She was faking the whole thing, so *she'd* be the first person on Mars."

"Alex..."

"Come on. She knows that's when we do the pressure checks. When we're in the engine room with no way of hearing her open the door." His tone turned acrid. "You have a little crush on her, and it's clouding your judgment. Wake up and see it for what it is."

"You weren't the one sitting with her half the night," he shot back. "She *wasn't* faking it. I tried everything. She wouldn't say a word to me. Just kept muttering in Polish." He sucked in a breath. "I'm going to try contacting her radio."

Blip. "Jayne? Jayne, are you there?"

Faint static came through my headphones.

"She's not responding."

"So let's go," Alex replied.

The familiar *th-thunk-creeeeak* of the ship's door opening.

A few minutes of heavy footsteps and breathing followed. So quiet, I could hear the sound of the cassette tape spinning.

Then George's voice cut back in.

"We've followed the footprints about 500 meters. They've gotten... er, more erratic. Swerving back and forth. We haven't found Jayne yet."

"We've come across some trenches that suggest ancient volcanic activity," Alex added. "While George searches for Jayne, I'm going to take some soil samples for the lab."

"You're not coming with me?"

"I'm going to do my job," Alex said flatly.

"Your *job* is to protect your crewmates."

"Not when they've betrayed you."

A shuddering sigh. A few minutes of crunching footsteps, as George set out on his own. Then—*blip*. "Jayne, if you can hear me, please say something. We're looking for you. We're worried."

Faint static—but this time, it was slightly different. The volume increased and decreased, slowly, rhythmically.

"Breathing. She's breathing. She's alive!" I could hear the tears in George's voice, and it made my heart break. "Jayne, answer me. Are you okay? Do you need help?"

No answer.

Chills ran down my spine. I swallowed, staring at the cassette player sitting on my desk. *I'm not sure I want to listen to the rest of this.* There was a reason we never heard about Andromeda Two. Why it was kept a secret, why the records were locked in a basement closet...

George's breathing filled my headphones as he began to run. I could picture him—the man I saw in the photo—running in an astronaut suit, following Jayne's footprints in the Martian desert. I bit my lip, praying he found her and they were both okay, even though this had happened 30 years ago and their fates were already sealed.

"Jayne! Oh, there you are, thank God!"

Silence.

"Jayne? Why are you hiding back there?"

No reply.

"Come on out, so we can get you back to the ship."

Blip. "Alex, I found her. She's hiding between this little crag in the rocks... for some reason. She won't come out. Can you come join us? I'm a few hundred meters from where we split. Right by the mountain."

An exasperated sigh. "Okay, *Captain*," he said, his voice dripping with animosity. "I'll join you."

"Thanks. Jayne, come on out of there," George called out. His voice was happy, unconcerned, but I couldn't stop the horrible pit of dread forming in my stomach. *Why is she hiding?*

Why would she leave the ship in the first place, when she seemed terrified?

Several minutes followed of the same. George calling out, taking a few footsteps, and no reply. Sometimes I'd hear the familiar *blip* of the radio, and then Jayne's breathing. But she never said anything.

Then Alex's voice cut through.

"I'm here. Where is she?"

"I... I can't find her," he said reluctantly. "She was *right here,* I swear. But as soon as I got close she disappeared behind the rocks and now—I can't find her. I don't know if she slipped through this crack here... it looks too narrow, but she's so skinny. Her suit is like three sizes smaller than mine. Do you see anything?"

A rustling sound, then a *click.* I pictured a flashlight being flicked on, sweeping a dark Martian cavern, and shuddered.

"No. I don't see her."

Alex and George started to argue. It seemed to go on

for a while, so I fast-forwarded in short bursts. Finally, George's voice came through, defeated.

"It's getting dark... so we're going back to the ship."

The two of them walked in silence. Nearly a half hour of footsteps crunching on sand and rock. Finally, I heard the metallic scrape of a boot, a low creak, and a *thud*.

They were back inside the ship.

"October 27th, 1993," George's voice came through the headphones. Flat, low, devoid of emotion. "Jayne Kowalski is missing from our crew. She left two hours before dark, while we were performing routine pressure checks. We spotted her several hundred meters from the ship, but she would not communicate with us in any way."

A sudden sniffle.

"Jayne isn't just a crewmate. She's the most amazing woman I know." His voice broke. "Funny. Creative. A light in the darkness. A star. And if we can't bring her home—"

"Captain," Alex cut in.

His voice was soft. Conciliatory.

"I'm sorry, George." Sniffling sounds. "I think... I think you were right. She would've been back by now. But I think I know how to find her." A soft thump, followed by the rapid clacking of keys. "The heat maps."

"Oh, my God. Why didn't I think of that?"

"It's scanning now. We should know her exact location in a few minutes."

My heart pounded in my chest as the silence stretched on. I stared at the white, toothed gears of the cassette, spinning behind the plastic. *Find Jayne. Find her, find h—*

"Uh... that doesn't make any sense." Alex's voice.

"What?"

"It says... she's inside the ship."

A soft *thud* came through the headphones.

Then racing footsteps, across the floor. I could hear Alex calling out George's name, but his voice grew more distant with each footstep. I gripped the desk, my throat dry, my knuckles white—

"She's in here, Alex!"

Stumbling. Rustling.

"Jayne? Are you okay?"

A faint, weak voice replied with something I couldn't make out.

"Are you hurt?"

More unintelligible mumbling.

"George," Alex's breathless voice came through the headphones.

"I'm trying to—"

"*George!*" A loud rustling sound—as if Alex were grabbing him. Shaking him. "Listen to me, dammit. She hasn't left the ship. *She hasn't left the ship.*"

"What are you talking about?"

"Her suit is still gone."

The silence seemed to stretch on for hours. Then, finally, George spoke up in a weak, shaky voice. "What... what are you trying to say?"

"Whoever you saw out there in the rocks wasn't her."

"That's impossible. It was her radio. Her suit. Her—"

"I don't know how. Okay? I don't know. Maybe Jayne opened the door while we were doing our pressure checks. Maybe she let something in. Maybe it tricked her, maybe she thought it was one of us. But instead it took her suit and—"

"What are you implying?"

A pause.

"That we're not alone here."

The silence hung heavy in the air. And then my heart plummeted as I heard a familiar sound. A sound I'd heard many times over the span of this recording.

Th-thunk-creeeeak.

The sound of the door being opened.

Shouts erupted. "Lock the door!" "I have to secure the airlock—" *Clunk.* "It's too late!" "Stop—" *Thud!* "No—"

But over their shouting, I could make out a woman's voice. Jayne. She was muttering something in Polish, one word, over and over. *"Ciemność."*

And then, as the sounds grew to a deafening roar—

Click.

End of tape.

I stared at the player, my heart hammering in my chest. I swallowed and, hands shaking, pulled out the cassette.

Over the coming days, I poured myself into research on the Andromeda Two. I must've Googled each of the crew member's names a dozen times. But nothing ever came up. No obituaries, no missing persons reports, not even birth or marriage certificates.

It was like someone had erased all evidence of their existence.

I repeated *ciemność* into a translation website as best I could. After numerous attempts, it finally came up witht the translation: darkness.

I returned the files and cassettes to the locked closet. I went to my boss and told him I'd never even went down there. Just "hey, you assigned me this weird case, but I don't think it's supposed to be mine because it's not in the records room." His face went white and he thanked me, before shooing me out of his office to make a phone call.

But I can't forget what I heard. Especially now, when tech billionaires are claiming they'll send someone to Mars within the decade.

I know that we're never going back.

Because *it* is waiting for us.

MY HUSBAND DIES EVERY NIGHT AT 7:48PM

It first happened while we were waiting for the 7:48 subway home.

We were arguing. He'd been checking out the waitress at dinner, and while that wasn't something I should've picked a fight over, it was our *anniversary* dinner. I couldn't stop a few snarky comments from slipping out.

"Look, I'm sorry, okay? I don't know what else you want me to say," he said, as we huddled together on the cold platform. "I wasn't *trying* to check her out, like staring at her. It just *happened.*"

"Well it never *happens* with me, does it?"

"It did, all the time! When you were younger!"

When I was younger. I let out a low growl, like a primal animal, and stared daggers at him.

He took a few steps back.

His foot caught on a crumpled Burger King wrapper.

He slipped—

And then fell onto the tracks below.

The roar of the train. *Thunk, thunk, thunk.* The blinding lights. The blaring horn.

The metal flashed past, and I knew it was all over.

That night was the most miserable of my life. I screamed, I cried, and I felt like the most worthless human being in the universe. It was my fault. I'd picked a stupid fight. And now he was dead.

The police took my statement. Then I flopped down on the bed and stared at the ceiling, listening to the cars roll by. The soft tinkle of our wind chimes. The clatter of the dry branches in the wind.

I thought I would never fall asleep. Ever. But somehow, between the hours of 3 and 4, I must have passed out. Because the next thing I knew, I was waking up on a sunny morning.

With John sleeping next to me.

What the fuck?

He rolled over towards me and gave me a grin.

"Happy anniversary, babe."

I assumed it was a dream. Somehow. It was the only way I could justify what happened. A horrible nightmare that I thought I'd never escape from, but did.

"So our reservation at *Poulet* is at 6—"

"Cancel it," I said.

"Uh, what?"

"Cancel it. We'll stay in. I'll cook you dinner."

He looked at me and frowned. "Uh, okay. Sure. Saves us some money, why not."

That night, I spent hours in the kitchen frying chicken, roasting vegetables, and lighting candles. At 7:20 we sat down to dinner.

John took a bite of the chicken. "So Dan says, he needs me to finish it in an hour, or I'm fired. And I say—"

His eyes went wide.

"John?"

His hand shot up to his neck.

Oh, God, he was choking.

I ran over to him. Wrapped my arms around him and thrust my hands into his abdomen, attempting the Heimlich. Nothing. Smacked him on the back, shook him.

Nothing.

He slipped from my hands and fell onto the floor, skin white, eyes wide. Behind him, hanging on the wall, was our clock.

7:48 PM.

The next morning, I woke up to him beside me.

"Happy anniversary, babe."

I grabbed my phone of the nightstand. Checked the date. FEBRUARY 16. I slapped the phone back down.

The same day. Again. *How?*

"Excited for tonight?"

No. No, I'm really not.

"I heard *Poulet* is—"

"We're not going to *Poulet*," I snapped.

"Uh, okay. You want to get a pizza? Or eat at home?"

"Maybe we should skip dinner entirely."

"What?"

"I've been meaning to try this fasting thing. It's, uh... it's like a zen yoga thing. To commune with the universe and all that."

"Well, we can do that tomorrow—"

"No!" I shouted, sitting upright in bed. "Tonight. It has to be tonight."

He shrugged. "Okay. You feeling all right?"

It's some sort of nervous breakdown. A reaction to stress. Nightmares, hallucinations, whatever they were. It wasn't possible that I was living in some sort of perverted Groundhog Day. It just wasn't. My aunt Theresa had struggled with vivid hallucinations, of demons and angels and death. I must have inherited it from her.

"I'm fine," I replied.

Make appointment for psychiatrist, I noted to myself.

At 7:40, I "accidentally" locked John in the bathroom.

"Hey! Isabel! Can you hear me?!" His muffled voice filtered downstairs. "I accidentally locked myself in the bathroom!"

The bathroom's had a shitty latch since forever. I never thought it would actually come in handy.

"Isabel!"

I set John's fancy skillet on the stove. Oil bubbled and fizzled above the flame. I hummed to myself as I set down patties of ground beef, watching them shrink and darken. *Sorry, John,* I thought to myself. *This is for your own good.*

I glanced at the clock. 7:45.

"Isabel!"

Just a few more minutes...

I slid the spatula under the patties. One by one, I carefully flipped them over. They sizzled delightfully. I turned to the fridge and swung the door open—

Thump.

I bolted upright.

"John?" I shouted.

Nothing.

Oh God, oh God—

I raced up the stairs. It took me a few minutes to get the handle open, but when I did, it was a gruesome scene.

The floor was damp from my recent shower. Slippery. And there was John, lying across the cream tiles. His head leaned against the side of the tub, deep red pouring from the back of his head.

I began to scream.

"Happy anniversary, babe."

"John, um... we need to talk." I slipped my phone back on the nighstand, the screen glowing with the words FEBRUARY 16. "There's, uh, been something happening to me."

He frowned. "I don't understand."

"Every day... is February 16. And every day, at exactly 7:48 PM... I see you die." I waited for a reaction, a reply. But he just stared at me, his dark eyes wide with concern.

"At first I thought they were all nightmares. Really vivid ones. Then I thought I was hallucinating, like Aunt Theresa... because how could this be true? How could I be living the same day, over and over and over? But it all feels so real. I've been losing you, every night, for the past three days."

John reached out his hands and took them in mine. He squeezed them, softly.

"I can't take it anymore," I said, my voice starting to crack. "I can't keep watching you die, John. Whether it's real or fake. So I need to get help... or something... because I don't know what to do."

John didn't reply. He just kept his dark eyes on mine, his warm hands on my hands.

"John?"

"February 16," he said, his eyes never leaving mine. "Do you remember what day that is?"

"It's our anniversary."

"Anniversary... of what?"

I frowned. "I don't understand."

"You can't stay here, on this day, forever," he said, squeezing my hands in his. "I love you."

Then he leaned forward and pressed his lips against mine. I closed my eyes, losing myself in the kiss.

When I opened them—

I was lying in an empty bed.

The room was dark, thick curtains hanging over the glass. Only the faintest traces of morning sunlight filtered through. I jumped out of bed, my heart hammering in my chest.

"John? *John?!*"

But as I raced around the house—as I saw the closet, half-empty, the kitchen devoid of John's trusty skillet and sauces, the driveway without his trusty old Camry—reality slowly melted back to me.

February 16.

It wasn't the anniversary of our marriage.

It was the anniversary of his *death.*

Three years, now. Three years I'd been living in darkness, reliving his death. Not some horrific accident, some horrible death I couldn't prevent.

Just a long, hard battle with cancer.

I walked over to the window and pulled back the curtains. Opened the window. The cold winter air poured over me, through my gray hair and my thin pajamas.

"I love you, too," I whispered.

A TRUE CRIME PODCAST... ABOUT MYSELF

Every night on my walk home from work, I listen to true crime podcasts. Even though my favorite podcast already released their episode for this week, the app said there was a new one. Excited, I hit PLAY.

"It was a small town--the kind that still has Mom and Pop shops lining the street, the kind where everyone knows your name. But little did the residents know that they would soon be rocked by a horrible crime."

I stopped at a traffic light. The red glowed in the darkness, glinting off the wet street. A black SUV sloshed by. Across from me, eerie blue refrigerator lights glowed from inside a corner deli. The chairs all up on their tables, feet in the air.

The signal turned to WALK.

"That chilly September evening was no different for the young student. She'd left her shift at the local

store and walked back home... except she never made it home."

Young student. Local store. Damn, this was hitting close to home. I was a part-time student at Franklin Community College, and worked at the local convenience store.

And, of course, I was walking home.

I glanced behind me--looking at the alleyway behind *Alessandro's Pizza,* which was dark except for the neon light spilling from the sign.

"Her boyfriend reported her missing the next day. The town conducted a volunteer-led search, and after two days, they found something."

Dread formed in my stomach, anticipating "a body." But what he said next was so, so much worse.

"Washed up on the shore of Worthington Lake, they found a pair of size 9 red Converse sneakers."

I stopped.

And looked down at *my* red Converse sneakers, damp from the rain.

What the hell?

My heart began to pound.

"The shoes were sent to a forensic analyst, who would compare its wear pattern to another pair of her shoes to try and determine if they belonged to the victim."

A rumbling sound made me jump. I turned--to see a dark SUV turning left at the intersection. *Didn't I see that car a few minutes ago? Maybe it's following me, and—*

The car passed me and disappeared into the darkness.

Come on, Sarah. Get a grip. Converse are popular sneakers. A little out of fashion, but still. 9 is a common women's shoe size. And what college student *doesn't* have some sort of a job? What, you think you're listening to some sort of prophecy of your own death?

Yeah, right.

"After a few weeks, the results came back. The analyst was certain: the shoes belonged to none other than Sarah Campbell."

The blood drained from my face.

Sarah Campbell.

My name.

What the fuck? How--

I didn't have time to think. I forced myself to move. I broke into a run. The small shops turned into a colorful blur.

"Searching the lake came up empty. Without a body, a crime is hard to solve. But police didn't give up. And finally, a witness came forward: someone had seen a car parked at the lake that night, around 2 AM. A black SUV with darkened windows."

No, no, no.

What the hell is going on?

I whipped around. The street was empty. No people, no cars. *No witnesses,* said the little voice in the back of my mind, the one that's watched way too many true crime shows. My eyes scanned the shops. All closed.

"There were six black SUVs matching the witness's description in the Franklin area. But one of them, in particular, caught Detective Nolan's eye. It belonged to Jon Kelly... a registered sex offender."

Vrrrm.

The sound was so soft I almost didn't hear it over the voice of the podcast. I whipped around—and there it was. Two blaring-white headlights behind me.

Coming from a black SUV.

I forced my legs to pump faster. The car didn't speed up; it crawled along, slowly, taking its time. Like the driver knew he could catch me, no matter what. I glanced back, trying to make him out behind the darkened windshield—but the headlights were too bright to see anything.

"Kelly wasn't just *a registered sex offender. He'd been convicted of assaulting a woman he worked with... who had multiple piercings and short dark hair, just like Sarah."*

The car crawled down the road. Stalking me, like a lioness stalks her prey. I veered left, onto our dark residential street.

Just a few more steps.

Headlights flashed across me, illuminating my running shadow on the pavement. I didn't look back. I just ran, as fast as I possibly could. The little brown house with the yellow shutters came into view. I sprinted across the grass, grabbing my keys from my pocket.

Click.

I threw the door open--and slammed it shut behind me.

Then I turned the deadbolt, collapsed against the door, and began crying.

I heard the *rush* of the car passing our house, continuing down the road. But I wasn't safe—Gabe wasn't home yet. I was alone, in a dark house, with someone driving down the street who knew exactly where I lived.

Still sobbing, I checked all the locks. Then I called Gabe, who assured me he was five minutes away.

I made my way down the dark hallway and headed into the bathroom. Then I set my phone on the counter, grabbed a clump of tissues, and began to blow my nose.

Click.

I jumped. Whipped around.

But it wasn't coming from outside the door. My phone's screen lit up--the podcast was still playing. I must have hit it when I put the phone down. It had skipped several minutes forward, according to the play indicator.

"What do you think happened to Sarah?" the baritone voice asked.

I reached for it, to turn it off—

"Well, she'd told me she wanted to run away before."

I stopped dead.

It was Gabe's voice. Clear as day, coming from the speakers.

"She did? Why?" the voice asked.

"She wasn't happy with her grades, her job, her parents. She told me sometimes she'd dream of just... moving to some random state and leaving it all behind."

I froze, staring at the mirror.

I never said that. Never.

Gabe... was lying?

"I mean, that was hurtful to me as her boyfriend, you know? I thought we were going to get married someday. But apparently she didn't feel the same way."

My heart pounded in my ears.

"So you think she just skipped town, and is happily living her life out somewhere else? Rather than being abducted or murdered?"

A pause.

"Yes. That's exactly what I think."

"That's all for now! Thank you to our listeners..."

The outro played. I stared at my reflection, everything coming down all at once, my mind trying to race and catch up with what it meant—

The front door creaked open. Footsteps sounded outside.

"Sarah! I'm back!"

I backed away from the door.

"Sarah?"

My eyes fell on the window. I ran over to it, turned the lock. *Push*—I popped the screen out.

Then I swung a leg over, pulled myself through the window, and ran as fast as I could.

The nightmares continue in...

YOU CAN'T HIDE
30 TALES BY BLAIR DANIELS

AVAILABLE NOW

I found a note I don't remember writing.
It says 'Don't look under the bed.'

"ATTENTION SHOPPERS: Please hide at the back of the store immediately."

I created a chatbot. It said some deeply disturbing things.

I was in a bus crash with five other passengers. After the crash, there were six.

YOU CAN'T HIDE brings you 30 terrifying tales for your darkest nights. This collection has every flavor of horror, from murderous husbands to malevolent doppelgangers, from terrifying photos to sinister board games. Read... if you dare.

———————————

Hungry for more horror? Visit www.blairdaniels.com or sign up for my newsletter.

Thanks for reading!

Printed in Great Britain
by Amazon